THERE'S ONLY
ONE
Sleigh

holiday h•e•a

NEW YORK TIMES BESTSELLING AUTHOR
SHANNON STACEY

She's a Scrooge from the city and he's a holiday-loving, small-town fire chief, but being thrown together to plan the Charming Lake Christmas Fair might land them on the naughty list.

Whitney

I'm not a fan of small towns or the distraction Christmas brings every year, but when my boss asks me to help with Charming Lake's annual Christmas fair, I see an opportunity to impress the man who holds my career in his hands. The plan is to be my usual focused and efficient self, get the job done, and get out. Then I meet the hot, funny guy in the Charming Lake Fire Department T-shirt and the plan blows up. Things get festive fast, but there's no way I'm giving up my city life for a man I've just met.

Rob

When my brother-in-law assigns his assistant to help me with the town's Christmas Fair, I want to tell him to pound snow, but he's a hard man to say no to. I don't expect a gorgeous, notebook-wielding woman to walk into my fire station and shake my life like a snow globe. I know I'm supposed to be focusing on the festival, but suddenly it feels like my only job is making Whitney laugh...and proving to her good things can happen in a small town.

If you're in the mood for a festive read full of love, laughter and happily ever after, the HOLIDAY HEA series is here for you!

CHAPTER
One

WHITNEY

There's nothing worse than Christmas in a small town.

Small towns look cute in the movies and, sure, sometimes I'll pause while scrolling if Instagram's algorithm inexplicably serves me a picturesque photo. There are probably hundreds of pictures of Charming Lake, New Hampshire online because it's definitely picturesque. Christmas wreaths and lights and inflatables are everywhere, and I think every single building has an electric candle in every single window.

I think Charming Lake could have spent a little less of the town budget on wreaths for every pole, and more on basic infrastructure—like a drive-thru coffee shop or having separate stores for eggs and wool socks instead of packing everything into one general store—but nobody asked me.

I'm also not a big Christmas person. I don't hate it or anything. There's no trauma. There's no childhood memory of the year I didn't get a doll I asked for and thought it was because I was on the *naughty* list. Christmas is just...super annoying. It's a distraction.

It's pretty enough on the surface—all white glitter and sparkling red garland—but the holiday is an invasive weed that spreads and chokes off regular life. The root system is so well-established, it's not even contained to the weeks between Thanksgiving and New Year's anymore. Now you wake up the day after Halloween and—*ho ho ho*—Merry Christmas.

After the holidays is one of the worst symptoms of the Christmas infection, and it's one of my least favorite phrases. Every year, though, I hear it a little earlier. Work is put on pause while people obsess over cookies and how to buy the perfect gifts for everybody they've ever met without taking out a second mortgage on their homes.

When it comes to work, I don't have a pause button. I don't defer matters of business in favor of building gingerbread houses. It's one of the reasons I went to work for Donovan Wilson. You don't become a billionaire by slacking for two months out of every year.

Donovan is technically a millionaire now, I guess, because he's giving so much money away, but that makes it even better. I can get the experience I need while working for a man I respect. Thanks to Donovan's executive assistant going on maternity leave, I finally have a chance to stand at his side and prove myself. Even if the position is temporary, it'll go on my resume, along with an excellent recommendation from the boss. I know it'll be excellent because that's the standard I hold myself to.

But Donovan got stranded in this small town by a winter storm just before Christmas a few years ago and fell in love with a local. And somehow I've been tasked with being his liaison with the town committee and acting as *their* assistant to ensure Charming Lake's Christmas celebration is the best it can be.

Christmas in Charming Lake.

It sounds like the title of a horror movie, and I'm the

lingerie-clad co-ed being sent into the basement without a flashlight.

I'm actually being sent to the fire station, which feels like a weird place to have a meeting. I assumed we'd have a meeting room at the town hall, which is definitely a lot easier to find than the fire station. I think I've passed that front porch with the bear carved out of wood on it three times, but it's hard to tell because there are a lot of wooden animals in this town. And a lot of front porches.

I knew public transportation was out of the question, but I assumed they'd have the bigger rideshare options. I should have guessed from the way Donovan chuckled as he tossed me the keys to a small all-wheel-drive car that this would be an adventure.

Okay, I've definitely seen that inflatable Nativity set at least twice. How is it so hard to navigate a town this small?

Maybe I should just set something on fire and let them come to me.

CHAPTER
Two

ROB

Rich people are a pain in the ass.

I know this because my sister married one. And then the guy Natalie married sent his assistant to assist *me* and I don't seem to get a say in the matter. Actually, I do have a say because I'm in charge of the Christmas fair this year, but my entire family pressured me to let Donovan do this *favor* for me, so here I am, waiting for an assistant I don't want who's supposed to help me with things I don't need help with.

Because, again, rich people are a pain in the ass.

A sound distracts me and it takes me a few seconds to place it—the authoritative clack of high heels on the cement floor. It's not something I hear around the station very often. There's nobody else around, so I leave my office and walk to the top of the stairs that lead down to the equipment bay.

The woman standing between the ladder truck and my red SUV has her hand on one hip and the other is holding a black satchel. Black seems to be the theme—black hair flowing down her back, black business suit with a skirt that shows off stunning legs, and black heels that make sure I don't miss those legs.

She's definitely not from Charming Lake. There's no way I would forget having seen her before.

My battered leather work boots aren't quiet on the wood steps as I descend the stairs to find out what she wants. She looks up and the overhead lights hit her hair differently. It's not black, just a really dark brown, and her eyes are a light brown.

"Can I help you?" I ask when I reach the bottom.

"I'm looking for Rob Byrne."

While that would explain why this woman is in my fire station, I still can't wrap my head around why she's looking for me at all. She looks like a lawyer. Is somebody suing the fire department? Sure, Mrs. Hoover was really upset we ruined her flower garden back in August, but we were trying to put out the fire in her kitchen at the time. Even for her, a lawsuit seems like an extreme level of crankiness, and not a proper thank you for the fact we saved the rest of the house.

Then it hits me—*she's* Donovan's assistant. This is the woman he sent to help me, even though I told him not to.

"That's me," I tell her.

Her scowl deepens, and she tilts her head slightly. "You're Rob Byrne?"

"Yup. Still me."

"Sorry, I was expecting—"

Her words cut off and she takes a deep breath while I wonder what she'd been about to say. She was expecting somebody older? Younger? Taller? Somebody dressed in a suit like my brother-in-law wears, sitting at a conference table?

"I'm Whitney Forrester," she says, shifting her coffee cup to her left hand so she can extend her right. "I work for Mr. Wilson, and he decided I'll be helping you with the Charming Lake Christmas Fair this year."

He decided. The way she phrases that isn't lost on me, and I wonder if she thinks this situation is as ridiculous as I do. When she withdraws her hand, I realize I'd held on to that handshake a few seconds more than necessary.

"I apologize for being late, but my phone's GPS didn't seem to be accurate," she continues, talking fast. "And directions like 'take a right after the old feed store' would be more helpful if the old feed store hadn't—according to the third person I asked for directions—burned down when I was seven years old."

"Sorry about that. We've been trying to get that GPS issue fixed so out-of-towners stop getting lost, and so we won't have to rescue anymore cars from the snowmobile trail their phones told them to take, but it's an ongoing process."

She takes a quick breath and straightens her spine even more before pasting on a fake smile. "Well, I'm here now and ready to get started."

I wonder what it would take to make her *really* smile. She's here to help me plan this year's Christmas fair, but that doesn't mean I can't make a little side quest out of making Whitney Forrester smile.

"We'll be outside a lot. Did you bring boots with you?" I like the way her nose wrinkles when I say the word *outside*.

"I brought boots, yes, though planning is more of an indoor activity."

The planning is, but the execution is not. I'll probably keep that to myself for now, though. "Real winter boots? Or boots that look cute with your outfit?"

"Cute? I don't do *cute*, thank you." She doesn't smile. "I packed appropriate footwear for this trip. My mistake was thinking the Christmas fair *committee* would meet in an actual committee meeting room."

My brother-in-law might be a suit-wearing pain in my ass, but he's actually a really great guy. When he puts his phone down and closes his laptop, he's warm and funny and madly in love with his family. But I have a hard time seeing this woman putting her phone down and being warm and funny. If I asked her to hold a snowball, I probably wouldn't have to worry about it melting.

"Committee?" I chuckle, even as I start plotting some way to get back at Donovan for this. "I've been called a lot of things before, but never a committee."

"There's no committee?" The icy mask slips, leaving confusion and maybe some anxiety in its wake. "It's just you?"

"Just me," I confirm. "If you're looking for the Christmas fair committee, I'm your guy."

CHAPTER
Three

WHITNEY

I'm a confident woman. I'm smart, I'm very good at my job, and people find me physically attractive. But right now I feel like I just walked into a middle school cafeteria wearing all the wrong clothes and I'm about to slip on spilled ketchup.

This is not at all what I expected.

I'm your guy.

I know what he meant, but the phrase echoes through my body, pinging a whole lot of nerves I'd rather not have pinged right now.

In my world, men wear layers. Even the most impeccably cut suit covers everything from the neck down. Sure, sometimes a guy will take the coat off and roll his shirt sleeves up, showing off some forearm, but mostly it's all left to the imagination.

Looking at Rob Byrne doesn't tax my imagination one bit. A dark blue T-shirt bearing a CLFD logo hugs his body as though it was painted on him this morning. His dark uniform pants are snug, and his feet are shoved into old, unlaced leather work boots that are broken down in a way that makes me think he just steps in and out of them as necessary.

He has thick brown hair and really dark eyes, and there's nothing about him that's my type. Literally nothing. He's also my boss's brother-in-law.

I need to get this meeting back on track, so I lift my computer bag slightly. "Should we set up my access to documents pertaining to the Christmas fair? I have all of the most common programs and platforms on my laptop. Do you use Google Docs? Airtable?"

He snorts and then gestures up the stairs. "I have the information in my office if you want to see it."

"It would probably be helpful." His eyebrows shoot up at my dry tone, but my feet are freezing and starting to ache from standing on a cement floor in heels. But this man will be reporting on my performance to Donovan, even if it's casually over a family dinner, and I force a smile. "After you?"

He hesitates and I know he's thinking *ladies first*, but if I try to walk up those stairs with Rob Byrne eye-level with my ass, I'll be so self-conscious, I'll probably fall and take him down like a bowling pin.

He finally goes first, but he pauses on the second step. "Be careful on these stairs. I'm pretty sure they grabbed some old barn boards to build them back in the 1800s and never replaced them."

"Unsafe stairs in a building dedicated to public safety? That's a little ironic." It's probably for the best, though, because having to look where I'm stepping keeps me from staring at *his* ass all the way to the top.

"Replacing them is on the list, but every time a little money shakes loose from the budget, it goes to something more important. Equipment or training, usually."

At the top of the stairs, he takes a right into a room that's so cluttered, I might actually break out in hives. There's a desk covered in papers and a computer that might be older than I am, and a table covered with…stuff. A narrow bed with a duffel bag on top. Does he sleep in here? A large window overlooking where the trucks are parked and a window over the table keeps the space from being claustrophobic, but it's obvious the man spends a great deal of time in here.

After rummaging through a drawer in a gray metal filing cabinet that might be older than both of us combined, Rob turns and hands me a three-ring binder so fat and overstuffed with papers—many of them not in the rings—I have to use both hands to take it from him. It's the kind of binder that has a clear vinyl sheet on top so a cover can be inserted, but it's so tattered and taped, it's hard to make out the words typed in a large font.

Charming Lake Christmas Fair.

I look up at him. Is that amusement I see around his eyes and mouth? He looks like he's trying not to laugh at me. "What is this?"

"The Christmas Fair binder. You said seeing it would *probably be helpful.*"

I'm too horrified by the object in my hand to react to his unflattering imitation of me. "I meant something from this century."

He leans back against the table and crosses his arms in a way that draws attention to the bulge of his biceps under his T-shirt sleeves. "Has anybody ever told you that you're very judgmental?"

My cheeks burn, and I'm not sure if it's from the insult or the extreme effort it takes me not to stare at his forearms. "I apologize for coming across that way. What I am is very good at my job and that's due in large part to my excellent organizational skills and efficiency. This is…neither."

I'm really making a horrible first impression, so I keep talking before he has the chance to throw me out. "I think a good use of my time right now would be taking this back to the inn and becoming familiar with the material, so I can have a clearer picture of the event, what goes into it, and how I can best assist you with the planning."

He's shaking his head before I even stop talking. "That's not just a messy binder of information. It's like an archive of sorts—a history of the event. Some of those notes are pretty old, and the people who wrote them aren't with us anymore."

The way Rob looks at the binder sends a strange and very unwelcome warmth through my body. When the lines of his face soften and a sentimental smile plays with the corners of his mouth, he's even more handsome.

I need to get out of here—with or without the binder. Preferably with, though, because Donovan's going to ask me how this went and I don't want to tell him my dislike of holiday festivities and an inexplicable attraction to his brother-in-law threw me off and nothing got accomplished.

"I'll take excellent care of it," I promise. "I know I don't really fit in here, but I can tell you I'm good at my job and right now, my job is to help you put on the Charming Lake Christmas Fair."

He blows out a breath as he runs a hand through his thick hair. My fingers tighten on the binder. "Look, Whitney. This is my first time being in charge of the fair, and because Sophie—she ran it for at least the last fifteen years—asked me personally to take it over, I'm feeling the pressure. I *know* you're good at your job because Donovan told me you are, but this isn't about software and data and efficiency. The Christmas fair is about tradition and community and holiday festivity the Charming Lake way."

Panic claws at my gut, but I do my best to give him a reassuring smile. I can't lose this opportunity to work on something meaningful to the boss. "Maybe we'd make a good team, then, because between the two of us, we bring to the table everything we need to plan the best Christmas fair that Charming Lake has ever seen."

After a long moment of silence broken only by my heart beating and the hum of the station's HVAC system, Rob grins.

And yup, he's even *more* attractive.

"You might be right," he says, much to my relief. "But just to be clear, the fair is always supposed to be a little better than the year before, but also fundamentally the same."

"Right. Tradition and nostalgia and all that," I say. "Generational memories all blending together."

"Just take good care of that," he says, dipping his head toward the binder I'm still holding. "I'll be around tomorrow all day, but you should know that I rarely get through anything without being called out."

"You're not the only one, are you?"

"I'm often the only one actually in the station, but we're a volunteer department. If a call comes in that requires a full response, the rest of them will leave whatever they're doing and show up."

Suddenly I have so many questions I want to ask. Does he sleep here every night, or does he have a home he gets to visit occasionally? Is there a reason he chose to be a firefighter in his hometown? Does he secretly want to leave Charming Lake behind and join Boston Fire or some other city's larger and presumably more exciting department?

Does he have a wife? A girlfriend? Kids?

"I'll get started on this right away," I say quickly, before I can go down that conversational road. "Thanks for this information, and I can see myself out."

"Careful on the stairs," he calls after me.

It's hard to make a quick or graceful exit when navigating ancient barn boards in heels, but I make it to the bottom without humiliating—or hurting—myself. And then I force myself to walk across the cement floor to the exit door without looking back to see if Rob's watching me through that window.

CHAPTER
Four

ROB

I stand in front of the table in my office, looking through the massive sheet of safety glass that lets me watch over the equipment bay. Right now I'm watching Whitney Forrester walk toward the door and listening to her heels click on the cement floor.

She walks as if she runs the entire world, which I didn't realize is something I find sexy until right now.

If only she wasn't my brother-in-law's assistant—and presumably an employee Donovan values if he brought her here to Charming Lake.

And then there's her attitude. Whitney's clearly a city girl who wants nothing to do with our town, our celebration, or even the holiday in general. She's all business and that's definitely not my vibe.

I snort, turning away from the window as the door closes behind Whitney. I don't think I even *have* a vibe anymore. The fire department, my family, and our community take up all of my time and energy. Over the last couple of years, I've lost interest in casual dating and hookups, but it's hard to make space in my life for finding a woman I can share a future with.

That's definitely not Ms. Scrooge with the leather satchel and snappy heels. She made it pretty clear she wouldn't darken Charming Lake's doorstep if Donovan hadn't given her the assignment. Any effort she put in would be to please her boss and not from a sense of community or holiday spirit. Granted, it's not *her* community, but she could pretend, at least.

I wait long enough for Whitney to have settled in her car and driven away before grabbing what I need and hitting the button to raise the overhead door. There's a pickup sitting in my driveway at home, but I usually drive the red SUV I was issued when I became the fire chief because it has the lights and sirens and equipment I need to respond from anywhere.

The drive to my sister's house involves returning the waves of almost every local I pass, either on the road or on the sidewalk, but eventually I turn onto the road that follows the lakeshore. About a mile down on the left is the house Donovan and Natalie bought and renovated.

I thought, when they bought it, Donovan would tear down the three-bedroom Cape that had been in that spot for a century and replace it with some glass and steel monstrosity. But he'd kept the original bones and lines on the exterior, other than larger windows, and stuck to cosmetic work. They'd gutted the inside, though, updating pretty much everything. But driving by and seeing the old historic lake-front property so lovingly restored was one of the reasons I'd decided Donovan Wilson wasn't so bad for a rich guy.

When he's not being a pain in my ass, of course.

I'm not surprised when he opens the door before I've even touched the doorbell. One, it might be discreet, but a top-notch security system was one of the upgrades. And two, when a man has a rambunctious child and a very pregnant wife, he doesn't let the doorbell ring.

"Hey, come on in," he says, stepping out of the way so I can enter.

I step out of my boots, nudging them off to the side, where there's an existing pile of footwear. Then I drop my coat on top. There's a coat closet, but I'm not going to be here long enough to fuss with it.

Usually my three-year-old nephew would have run into the hall and thrown himself into my knees with so much enthusiasm it literally staggers me by now. "Where's Sam?"

"He laid down on the living room floor with a book and fell asleep. I know I should move him, but he's so quiet and it *is* a really soft throw rug."

I follow Donovan into the living room, and decline a beverage when he offers one. I point at his chest instead. "Listen. I thought you and I were good."

"I thought so, too. Are we not good?" He shakes his head. "If we're not, you're the one telling your sister, and I don't want to be in the room when you do."

"I heard that," Natalie calls from the hallway a few seconds before walking into the room.

I stand and lean in over her very substantial baby "bump" to kiss her cheek. "Hey, sis."

"Why are you two not good?" She asks, lowering herself onto the couch.

"I'm not sure," Donovan says as he sits next to her. I sink into one of the matching chairs. "Rob?"

"I'm not sure, either. You tell me what I did to you that was so bad you had to put Whitney Forrester in my life as payback."

He stares at me for a few seconds and then laughs in my face. Nat's laughing, too, and I might have enjoyed their amusement if it wasn't at my expense.

"She's intense," Donovan admits. "But she's excellent at her job."

"So she said." I snort. "More than once, I think."

"Whitney helping you was actually my idea," Natalie confesses, her cheeks still pink from laughing.

My own sister did this to me? "Is this because of that time I used a Sharpie to draw mustaches and beards on all your Barbie dolls?"

Donovan was sipping coffee and we both look at him as he almost chokes. He manages to swallow it without spitting it all over us, so Nat turns back to me with narrowed eyes.

"I'll never forgive you for that," she says. "But no. This is your first time in charge of the Christmas fair, and Whitney is excellent at managing things. Take the help, Rob."

"This might be the first time I've been in charge, but I've been attending the thing my whole life. And I've actually been in on the planning for several years. I've got this."

"She'll just help you *got this* more efficiently," Nat says.

Donovan clears his throat. "There's also…well, I like Whitney and I've been a little worried about her. She's very driven, which is a good thing, but I don't think she has a lot of family. And I get the impression the holidays are hard for her. She's very disconnected from the whole festive vibe, and I'm hoping this will help her remember work isn't everything. Maybe because I used to be her, until I met Natalie, I see her going down that same road."

"I'm sorry," I say. "Are you implying I'm supposed to be her Jacob Marley?"

"Absolutely not," Donovan replies. "You should definitely *not* sneak into Whitney's room in the middle of the night, rattling your chains and making weird noises."

Natalie snorts. "Way to make it awkward, honey."

I laugh, but me sneaking into Whitney's room in the middle of the night was a suggestion my imagination does *not* need. I can still see the way her hips swayed, bumping the computer bag slung from her shoulder, as she walked out of the station.

"You love the fair," Nat says. "There's no better person to show her just how *charming* Charming Lake can be at Christmastime."

"Maybe take that up with Santa, because you're asking for a Christmas miracle."

CHAPTER
Five

WHITNEY

I manage to find my way back to the Charming Inn—my home for the next two weeks—with only one wrong turn. And it's hard to miss, being a massive, historical home over-looking the lake.

There aren't any other vehicles in the guest parking, so my fellow visitors must be out and about. I haven't met them, since I'm adept at avoiding the social areas during peak chatting time, but I know there's a young child who loves to sing in one of the rooms, and a couple that doesn't seem to like each other very much in another. Neither says *relaxing vacation* to me, but it's irrelevant. I'm here to work.

I sling my computer bag over my shoulder and then, being very careful not to drop any of the papers stuck haphazardly between the covers, I grab the binder from the passenger seat. Once it's tucked securely in my arm, I grab the fresh coffee I bought from the cupholder and go inside. Penny steps into the room when she hears the door. According to Donovan, whose in-laws own this place, Penny

—who looks to be in her fifties, with pale blonde hair and curves for days—was hired to run the inn after Donovan swept Natalie off her feet and she wanted to travel with him more than she wanted to mind the family business.

"Welcome back, Miss Forrester," Penny says. I tried to get her to call me by my first name when I checked in yesterday, but apparently that's not her thing.

"Thank you. I'm probably going to spend the rest of the day working in my room." I step out of my heels and, mindful of the binder and my coffee, crouch to hook my fingers in the backs of them.

"Let me know if you need anything," she says before going back to whatever she'd been doing.

I make my way through the inn to the staircase. It's lovely, as inns go, I guess. A nice balance of class and comfort without being too fussy. There are four rooms on the second floor, and an ADA accessible room on the first floor. And Penny's space is on the third floor. I usually stay in hotels when I travel because nobody expects you to make small talk with strangers, but the Charming Inn is…well, it's actually quite charming.

Once I'm behind my closed door, I place the binder on the bed, drop my shoes, and set the coffee and my bag on the small table I'm using as a desk. I sigh in relief as I unzip the skirt and step out of it. The blazer and shirt get tossed over the arm of the chair, and then I pop my earphones in.

In my camisole and briefs, I crank up the music and dance it out. Not wildly, of course. I don't want Penny to wonder what I'm up to, but I move my body to two high energy songs before I take a really deep breath and slowly exhale.

It's a habit I discovered during my first internship in college, when I had trouble transitioning from work time to not-working time. Not that there was a lot of time off then— or *now*, to be honest—but the only way I could not burn out was to be more deliberate about relaxing. Stripping off the business armor and a few minutes of dancing lets my body know we're done with the serious stuff and now we can chill.

I stick my earphones back in their case and make a quick trip to the (thankfully) ensuite bathroom before grabbing my coffee and notebook from the desk. The cup I set on the nightstand to keep it away from the binder, but the notebook I toss next to it. Then I sit cross-legged on the bed and open the cover.

Rob wasn't lying. The collection of papers, photos, invoices, and clippings is more a history of the event than an instruction manual. Bits of newspaper that are yellowed and crisp. Pages with torn holes that can't be fastened in place.

I'm pretty sure the notes on the thin paper I'm holding right now were written with a fountain pen.

It doesn't take long for my hyperfocus to kick in—my brain loves a challenging task—and I sort everything into categories first. There are lists and instructions and other papers relevant to the organization and running of the event. Then there are newspaper clippings and photographs that serve more like a chronicle of the Christmas Fair over the years. I do my best to sort the former by priority and the latter by date.

I need plastic sleeves to hold some of these in the binder, I think. And also some of those adhesive reinforcements for the punched holes that have torn.

My phone rings—or more accurately, my smartwatch vibrates to let me know my phone is silently ringing—and I snatch up my earphones when I see Donovan Wilson's name on the screen.

I pop in an earphone as I slide the screen to accept the call. "Hello, Mr. Wilson."

"How did everything go today?"

"I think it went well. Mr. Byrne gave me the information he had regarding the fair and I just finished going through it. I'm currently organizing my thoughts—" Or a hundred years' worth of the random thoughts of strangers, anyway. "—and I'll be ready to go when we reconvene tomorrow."

Did he just chuckle? It sounded like a chuckle. What did his brother-in-law tell him? "I'm glad to hear it. I'm sure Rob will appreciate the help."

I'm still not sure about that, but I don't make it a habit of contradicting the guy who signs my checks—or employs the department that triggers the automatic deposit of my salary, I guess.

"I'm glad to be of assistance," is all I say.

"Let me know if you need anything at all from me, and I'll touch base with you soon."

"Thank you, Mr. Wilson. Goodnight."

Now that my boss has yanked me away from the task I've been immersed in—and those stray thoughts about his wife's brother—I realize I'm hungry.

And when I open my favorite food delivery app, hoping to arrange for a bag of food to appear magically on the inn's front porch, I'm thankful there's no laughter sound effect to go with the *nope* the app gives me.

I'm going to have to venture out to get food, and if I'm going out, I may as well hit up the nearest office supply store. I always carry an extra charging cord for my laptop, but I haven't dealt with an analog workflow since high school.

After a search on my phone, I'm not surprised there aren't any office supply box stores in Charming Lake. I doubt the general store will have what I need, so it looks like I'm taking a field trip to the closest city.

CHAPTER
Six

ROB

Even though I've spent the entire morning thinking about the fact Whitney will be showing up at the station again today, I almost drop the wrench in my hand when she clears her throat right behind me. It's a very big wrench, and it would have hurt like hell if it bounced off my foot.

I set the wrench on the tool bench and turn, trying not to look like a man who just had a year taken off his life. She's not wearing her early warning high heels today, and I have the overhead doors open because it's an unseasonably nice morning, so she didn't have to use the visitor's door.

"Good morning," she says, handing me a large cardboard cup of coffee after double-checking that the one in her left hand has my name on it. "The woman at the General Store says this is how you like yours."

"Thank you." I take the hot cup, careful not to make contact with her fingers. "This is one of my favorite things about living in a small town."

"The coffee?"

She sounds incredulous, and I assume she's used to those fancy, foamy drinks that require a person to be fluent in a coffee language I don't speak in order to get some much needed caffeine. I still don't know the difference between a latte and a cappuccino, though to be fair, I haven't put a lot of effort into figuring it out.

"Not the coffee, though Beth makes a better brew than what we have here at the station," I say. "But the fact she knows how I take it, which means people can show up here with surprise coffee for me and I know it'll be right. And I can call the diner and ask for a burger to go and I don't have to go through all the details. They know how I like it."

The corners of her mouth tilt up. "And how is that?"

"Medium-well, with an extra slice of cheese, mayo and pickles. What about you?"

"Medium, with the regular amount of cheese, mayo and tomato. And ketchup for my crispy fries."

I shake my head. "Salt and vinegar on my fries."

"Vinegar?" I expect her nose to wrinkle, but she considers it for a second. "Interesting. What kind of vinegar? Apple cider? Balsamic?"

"Just plain white vinegar. We'll have to hit the diner while you're in town."

"It's a..." She pauses for a noticeable second. "Good idea. We can eat and plan at the same time. Very efficient."

Date. That was the word she didn't say, which strikes me as odd because it's a common enough phrase.

She holds the binder out to me before I can think of a response, and I'm not surprised there are no longer papers sticking out of it every which way.

"I scanned the contents," she says, "so I won't need to handle the originals again."

"Did you use that monstrosity of a printer at the inn? I tried it once, and every page has to be scanned one at a time."

"I have a scanner app on my phone that compiles the

documents and saves them as a PDF, which I then saved to my tablet so I can work from that copy instead of handling the binder."

Even with a fancy phone app, it must have taken her hours—first sorting and protecting the originals, and then the scanning of each individual page. "Tell me you didn't stay up all night doing this."

"I didn't stay up all night doing that."

I can't tell if she's trying to be funny or not. "Are you just saying that because I told you to say it?"

"No, it actually didn't take me all night, though I won't deny it was a lengthy process." She quirks an eyebrow at me. "Also, it's funny you think I'd do something just because you told me to."

If it's so funny, she should *smile*, dammit. Not her business lady smile, but a real one that makes her eyes sparkle.

"I'll also send you a copy of the PDF so you can archive it in the event something happens to the binder," she continues. "I know it's not quite the same, but at least it wouldn't be totally lost."

"That means a lot to me. Thank you." It means so much, actually, that I'm tempted to pull her into my arms and hug her, but I don't need a seminar to tell me that's crossing a boundary. "We can head upstairs and start triaging the list, I guess. Figure out what's a priority and what should have already been done days ago—if not weeks."

"Upstairs? In your office with one desk chair, one very uncomfortable looking wooden chair, and a bed?"

I'm confused for a few seconds—my brain cells scrambled by Whitney bringing the word *bed* into the conversation—and then I remember I didn't exactly give her a tour yesterday.

"We have a very small living area, too, which includes a table and chairs. I thought we could work there."

"Do you usually wait until two weeks before the event to start planning?"

"No. I usually get less than two weeks because I just do what I'm told and do the heavy lifting. And it's not as if Christmas is a surprise party. But Susan was running behind this year because of some health issues and she left her decision to retire and hand it off to me a bit late."

She lifts her hand, looking at the smartwatch on her wrist. Then she pulls out her phone and, after a moment of reading something, starts typing. I wait while she has what appears to be a text conversation with somebody.

"I'm sorry," she says, without glancing up. "With Mr. Wilson traveling tomorrow, I have a lot of balls in the air. Your Christmas Fair is on *top* of my duties to him as CEO, not in place of them. Even though everything's slowed down because we're in this whole holiday season thing now and everybody's distracted, doing it remotely from Charming Lake isn't easy."

"If the fair is too much, I can tell him I don't need your help."

She looks up from her phone, her eyes wide. "Please don't. It was an explanation, not a complaint."

Her voice is even, but there's a pleading look in her eyes. I only half-pay attention to my brother-in-law when he's talking about business, but I know Donovan's assistant is out on maternity leave because he grumbled about her and his wife being pregnant at the same time. Whitney's role in her boss's life is temporary, and she probably wants to leave as good an impression as possible.

"I'd tell him it's me and not you," I say, still wanting to give her an out if it's too stressful. "He'd believe that. Some people think I'm grumpy and prefer to be alone."

"You?" She *almost* smiles. "The man who put a bed in his office so he can hide behind the fire trucks?"

I laugh, shaking my head. "Hide? There's a giant glass window."

"I appreciate the offer, but I can handle this. It's not as if

I'm actually doing all the admin work from Charming Lake. I'm more of a liaison between Mr. Wilson and an entire department of people making sure he doesn't drop any balls."

"If you're sure." I gesture toward the stairs, trying not to think about that bed in my office again. "After you."

CHAPTER
Seven

WHITNEY

"This is your dining room table?" The scarred, round slab of wood looks older than me—possibly older than my mother, even—and five ancient office chairs, some with arms and some without circle it. It all barely fits in the open space between a tiny kitchenette and the area that's filled by a leather sectional couch and a TV.

He snorts. "I'm not sure this qualifies as a dining room, but this is where we gather sometimes and eat a meal or do paperwork or play cribbage."

"It works for me." I set my bag and coffee on the table, in front of the least ragged-looking chair. Then I pull out a sheaf of papers I kept together with a binder clip. "These look like sign-ups to be in the parade. I also found a master document that appears to be the rules and a waiver of liability. What I don't see is completed and signed participation forms matching up with each one of the applications. Was this not done yet, or were some participants denied?"

"It's not done yet." He sinks into the leather office chair on the other side of the table, which I correctly assumed was his. After scrubbing his face with his hands, he nods. "That's a top priority. I can't decide the parade order until I know who's confirmed, I guess."

"Have these been vetted in any way? Are they all approved to participate, or does somebody have to go through them still? Needless to say, I'm not familiar enough with your town to know if you have any bad apples."

"Every town has bad apples, but we rarely bounce anybody from the parade. Back in the late sixties, some people tried to get a nudist colony going on some land at the other end of the lake, and they were denied a float for obvious reasons. And the Little League team got a one-year ban after pitching candy to the spectators got a little competitive."

"The first clue would be that you toss candy. You don't *pitch* it."

"Yeah. Well, you know those fat, heavy Tootsie Pops?" When I nod, he smiles. "I had a wicked fastball, but the float was moving, so instead of hitting the guy who had a crush on my sister, his dad ended up with a bruise in the middle of his forehead."

I laugh, pointing at him. "*You're* one of the bad apples."

His eyes sparkle as he holds my gaze, his boyish grin taking my breath away. He grinned at me like that in my dream last night, right before he moved on to even more pleasurable activities. "They didn't complain when we brought home the trophy, though."

I want to hear more about what he was like growing up, but this isn't a date. It's a business meeting. "Okay, since this is a priority and we're both here, you take the stack of forms. Once you've made sure they're people who will wear clothing and toss candy instead of pitching it, you can hand it off to me. I'll make two piles—one for those who have signed the participation form and one for those who haven't."

We work for a while, drinking our coffees and listening to the soft strains of Christmas music coming from an unseen speaker. His phone rings several times, and I pause in my task to listen to him answering questions for whoever's on the other end. It's nice, I think, that the people of Charming Lake can get help from him without having to go through 9-1-1 or a non-emergency dispatcher. Then again, he probably *never* truly gets time off, because everybody in town probably has his cell phone number, too.

We're almost done with our task when his low, husky laughter draws my attention. He's looking at me, so I guess I'm the source of his amusement. "What?"

"Considering your lack of holiday spirit, you sure know every word to every Christmas song."

I hadn't realized I was singing along to the radio, and my cheeks grow hot. "My mom sings all the time, and she *loves* Christmas. Like, she's obsessed with it."

"And your dad?"

"He doesn't care about holidays, which isn't why they divorced when I was a kid, but probably didn't help. He does the tree and the gifts for Christmas, and he'll go to a Fourth of July barbecue, but he celebrates *on the day*. He doesn't let them distract him for the weeks leading up."

"I have to ask. Which parent did you prefer spending Christmas with when you were a kid?"

"I don't know. Mom was fun, but Dad had money, so there was so much food and don't even get me started on the gifts."

"Okay, wait. Is the reason you hate Christmas that you think your dad had money because he didn't let holidays distract him?"

I laugh. "That's ridiculous. One, I don't *hate* Christmas. I just think it's a…"

When I let the words trail away, his mouth quirks up at the corners. "Distraction. I think *distraction* is the word you were looking for."

"Don't be smug."

"Not smug. Just looking forward to you learning that celebrating the holidays with your community isn't a waste of time."

"Is this the part where you tell me I'll be visited by three ghosts in the night?"

His laughter echoes through the spartan space. "I'm going to ask Penny if you sit alone in front of the fireplace, eating gruel."

"Hey now, Bob Cratchit. I happen to like oatmeal."

"So the answer is yes."

I don't want to laugh and encourage his Dickensian nonsense, but I can't help it. Rob Byrne is funny and charming and, no matter how annoyed I am to be stuck in this small, holiday-loving town, I don't hate spending time with him.

Then he leans back in his chair and stretches, drawing my attention to the way his T-shirt molds to his flexing muscles. Some highlight reels from last night's dream flash through my mind, and I drop my gaze to the papers in front of me.

"Let's get back to work."

CHAPTER
Eight

ROB

The next morning, I stop at my sister's house before heading to the station. With Donovan heading out of the country, my entire family seems to be on edge.

He'll be back well before the baby's due, and Natalie made it very clear she'd rather he go now than go after the delivery, leaving her alone with Sam and a newborn. She and Donovan both feel good about the decision, but our mother and Lyla and Erin—my other sisters—are anxious about it.

Since my mother's car is in the driveway, so I know everybody's up and about, I let myself in without knocking. Sam sees me first and barrels into my knees.

"Uncle Rob!" I hoist him up with a groan because I'm pretty sure he's had a growth spurt in the few days since I last saw him, and I need to remember to lift with my knees.

After I kiss his cheek and he tells me in one long sentence that it's almost Christmas and his daddy's going on a plane and he had cereal with marshmallows for breakfast, he starts kicking to get down.

Then I lean down and kiss my mother's cheek. She's sitting on the couch, an affectionate look on her face as she watches her grandson. Mel and Elsa, Lyla's daughters, are ten and eight now, and Randy and Stella Byrne are thoroughly enjoying their grandparents era.

Sam shouting my name brings Natalie out of the kitchen and Donovan to the top of the stairs. My sister crosses to me and I kiss the top of her head while she hugs me.

"So what's *your* fictional reason for stopping by, giving you the opening to oh-so-casually mention I should stay at the inn or have somebody stay with me while Donovan's away?"

I laugh, but I don't bother to deny it. "Mom beat me to it, huh?"

"And you just missed Erin. Layla and the girls stopped by last night."

"You can't be mad at us, though."

"Oh, I'm not mad. But you all live within a five-mile radius of me, and if I don't feel good or I think Sam is too much, you know I'll call. Anyone of you would be here in minutes, and you know it."

"I have lights and sirens," I remind her.

"Save the lights and sirens for the parade because nobody in this house will need them," Donovan calls to him. "I'll be down in a few minutes."

"How is the planning going?" Natalie asks once I've taken my boots off and settled on the couch.

"Penny says Whitney is such a polite guest," my mom says before I can answer. "Spends most of her time working in her room, I guess, but she's very nice."

"She *is* nice, and I'm glad I have her to help me." Not just because she's good at her job, but because I look forward to working on the Christmas Fair so I can see her. I keep that part to myself, though. "She's very efficient."

Natalie wrinkles her nose. "Just how every woman wants to be described."

"I'm pretty sure Whitney would take it as a compliment. Her career is important to her."

"She's also quite pretty," my mom adds, and I groan.

She's actually gorgeous, not 'quite pretty,' but—again—keeping that to myself. "Don't get any ideas, Mom. She's only in Charming Lake because Donovan is here and because he offered her up to assist me. This isn't a place she'd *choose* to be."

My mom shrugs one shoulder. "Things change."

I'm having a hard enough time not getting any ideas of my own without my family playing holiday matchmaker. "Is Sam counting down the days until Santa comes?"

As expected, my nephew lights up and it's impossible to get a word in around the list of things he asked Santa for and what cookies he's going to eat and how many presents he's going to get. My mom gets suckered in by her grandson's excitement, but Natalie gives me a look that says she knows I derailed the conversation on purpose.

Maybe it's wrong to use Sam's holiday excitement against my pregnant sister, but I can't let Natalie get it into her head that I'm into Whitney. Even though only one of my sisters is married, all three of them are convinced I need a wife in my life.

My dad, who has sisters of his own, assures me this is typical sister behavior, so I should just smile and nod, but it's been a while since a single woman around my age showed up in Charming Lake. If I give off even the slightest vibe, this will turn into the matchmaking version of a shark feeding frenzy.

Sam keeps us distracted until Donovan comes downstairs, carrying a briefcase in one hand and a suitcase with the other. I don't even have to hear his footsteps on the stairs to know he's coming. Natalie's face softens and her eyes shine with love and contentment. It's an expression I only see when she looks at her husband or her son, and it always punches me hard in the chest.

I want that. I want to look at somebody like that, and I want to see it reflected back at me. Came close twice, I think, but the first woman I thought I'd spend the rest of my life with decided she wanted a life that didn't include erratic hours and fending for herself during storms. The second woman wanted a life that included a guy she met on the dating app she kept telling me she would *absolutely* delete.

It'll come. In the meantime, I have my family and my community. When I need a little extra gas in the emotional tank, time spent with Mel, Elsa or Sam does the trick.

"Whitney says I need to leave five minutes earlier than I planned," Donovan says, putting his bags by the door. "So I have ten minutes."

"Remember not to put your wallet and phone in your briefcase during the flight," Natalie reminds him.

"Losing my phone and wallet is what stranded me here with you." Donovan bends and kisses the top of his wife's head. "It's the best thing that ever happened to me."

"I'm going to head out," I say, pushing myself to my feet. I'll get out of the way so he can say goodbye to his family. "Natalie, if you need anything—no matter what it is—call me. Donovan, have a good trip. And Sammy, come give me a kiss. I have to go be the fire chief now."

My nephew makes siren sounds as he runs to me. The kiss and hug are rushed because he's more interested in his dad's imminent travel, though.

I kiss Natalie and my mom and then shake Donovan's hand before letting myself out. For my sister's sake, I wish they had longer to say goodbye today.

But for my sake? I can't wait for the man to be in the air so I can have Whitney back.

CHAPTER
Nine

WHITNEY

Other than grabbing a mug of coffee from the kitchen, I stay in my room with my phone and laptop ready until Donovan's jet is in the air. While he's known to send a lot of emails in flight, the urgency of any travel glitches is behind me until he lands and I can handle the flow of normal business communications from anywhere.

Like a fire station, I think as I pull on a blouse and top it with a pant suit. The way I keep anticipating seeing Rob again when every bit of my focus should have been on my boss is a little annoying, but a *lot* undeniable.

It's also really hard to deny it's *not* only because he's my partner in this opportunity Donovan has given me, since I had yet another very steamy dream about him last night. I woke up about four o'clock, flushed and aching, and I had a hell of a time going back to sleep.

Today's going to require a *lot* of coffee, so my first stop is the General Store. Beth looks unusually thrilled to see me, and when I try to give her my order, she holds up her hand.

"Wait. I want you to try something." Then she goes to the corner and I hear the coffee machine working. The last time I stopped in, she asked me questions about my usual coffee order when I'm at home, but considering the equipment she has at hand, I don't get my hopes up. I have no idea what she's making, but when she hands me an extra-large cardboard cup, I take it. "I think you'll like this one."

I take a sip, which feels awkward with her staring expectantly at me. Then I close my eyes and savor the sweet taste of *almost* perfect coffee before swallowing it.

"I can't believe you did this for me."

Beth scoffs, as if it's no big deal. "Good coffee makes people happy."

Since I'm smiling and she's currently one of my favorite people in the world, I can't deny it. "I appreciate this."

"How close am I? What do I need to tweak?" She waits, but this coffee is so good, I'm not about to complain. "Come on. Be honest with me."

"Maybe next time just a hair less sweetener," I tell her, but then I feel like an ass. "But it's practically perfect. This is delicious, I promise."

Beth grins, and then turns to spin a real honest-to-goodness Rolodex. After flipping through some cards, she pulls one out and makes a note on it. I'm curious how she has me filed since I didn't remember giving her my last name, and I lean in so I can read the top of the card upside-down.

Whitney from NYC.

"I can remake this one for you," she says after popping my card back into the Rolodex.

I clutch the precious cup to my chest. "No, you're not taking this from me. I'm going to savor it. You know those people who take the lid off and hold the cup up, getting every last drop? That's going to be me today."

Her cheeks flush with pleasure. "Are you heading to the

station? I can send a coffee along for the chief because the stuff they brew is an insult to the beverage."

I can't disagree, and when I finally find Rob in the kitchen of the firehouse, his entire face lights up. I wish it was for me, but his eyes are on the second coffee cup I'm holding. He reaches for it and takes a cautious sip.

"Thanks for this. And you have great timing. I was waiting on the library's list, and Erin dropped it off about a half-hour ago."

I know his sister is the librarian, but I'm still not sure what list he's referring to. Then he gestures toward a pile of papers with notes scrawled on them dumped on the table. Actually, there are *some* papers, along with a few sticky notes, an index card, and one envelope from an electric bill. There are a variety of toys, decorations, and candy, along with random other things written on them.

"What are these lists?" I look at the back of the envelope. "Individually wrapped candy canes not made of candy canes? I think that's what it says, but I'm not sure because the handwriting is atrocious and also it doesn't make sense."

"It's all Santa Fund stuff, and that's my list," he says sheepishly. "Those are candy canes to be prizes for the candy cane maze, but that activity is for the little ones, so they shouldn't actually be *real* candy canes. Do they make gummy candy canes?"

"I have no idea, but I can find out. Or maybe marshmallow ones?"

He points at me, grinning in a way that makes my skin feel hot. "Even better. That's how you problem solve."

"I'm sure I can find something online."

"Nope. The first step is your favorite thing—organizing for efficiency."

"It's not my favorite thing, you know. I'm just very good at it."

He leans forward. "What *is* your favorite thing?"

Your smile. The way your breath catches sometimes when you're watching me and don't think I can see you. Your forearms. Your ass. "Really good coffee."

Looking disappointed, he nods at the mishmash of papers I'm still holding. "I don't have a lot of free time today because of Fire Chief-type stuff, which is a lot less fun than Christmas. So if you can make some sense of those lists, we'll probably call it good until tomorrow."

I slide my laptop out of the bag. "It won't take me long."

"I have to lock myself in my office for a Zoom meeting in a few minutes. It shouldn't take more than thirty minutes if nobody goes off on any story-telling tangents, and then I'll check back."

There must have been at least a few stories because it's almost an hour before Rob emerges from his office. After a few false starts while I pushed the papers around, trying to decide how I want to sort them, I decided to group the items by which department they'd be found in if we were in a brick-and-mortar store.

I'm aware of him refilling his water tumbler and his sigh as he stands there waiting for the slow stream from the fridge's water dispenser. Then he sets the tumbler on the table and pulls a small notebook and pen out of his back pocket and tosses them beside it before sitting down.

Because it looks as if he might be jotting down some notes from his meeting, I'm quiet until he's done and clips the pen to the front cover of the notebook.

"Okay," I say, pushing back my chair. "The spreadsheet's sorted and color-coded. It's quite a list."

"It always is. Can you send it to the printer, please?"

"Why print it? I can go back to the inn and run the price comparison app I use to—"

"Nope. Just print it out."

"Okay. Then what do we do with it?"

"We shop." He swivels in his chair and gives me a grin that fills me with dread. "I have to meet some of the guys at the lake for a training exercise now, but I'll pick you up tomorrow morning at nine sharp. Oh, and you should wear comfortable walking shoes."

CHAPTER
Ten

ROB

Whitney's standing on the front porch of the inn when I pull into the driveway. Her spine is straight and her arms are crossed, and with three sisters and a few exes, I immediately recognize the body language of an annoyed woman.

It's eight minutes after nine.

By the time I put my truck in park, she's standing next to the passenger door, waiting for it to unlock. She climbs in without speaking and pulls her seatbelt across her chest, shoving it into the receiver with a little more force than necessary.

"I brought you a coffee for the road," I say, hoping caffeine will make up for the eight minutes of her life I squandered.

"Thank you." She picks up the cup on her side of the center console and takes a cautious sip. "It's perfect, just like yesterday's. Beth's been determined to make it just right and she nailed it. Did you just ask for whatever the annoying city girl likes?"

There's humor in her tone, which is a relief, and I chuckle. "I told her you and I are off to buy the presents and she made them both, no charge."

"She just *gave* you two free coffees?"

I'm starting to wonder if Whitney's ever had a role model who led with generosity and compassion because random acts of kindness seem to confuse her. "Everybody gives in different ways. The General Store can't donate the gifts and Beth can't close for a day to go shopping, but she can help fuel those who can."

"That's so nice." She takes another sip and smiles. "Speaking of closing for the day, did you put a notice on the Charming Lake Facebook Page forbidding anybody from having an emergency today?"

"First thing this morning. No using stairs or stoves or power tools, and a total ban on driving until I get back. I'm sure it'll be fine. Most people have Band-Aids and frozen peas, right?"

"Is this your truck?" she asks, looking around the interior. It rarely gets driven, so it's pretty immaculate—unlike the SUV I usually drive.

"No, I stole it from somebody's driveway because the fact I'm Fire Chief and my sister's ex-boyfriend is Charming Lake PD means I can't get in trouble for anything."

She almost spits a mouthful of coffee over the dash, which would have been messy, but also a win for me. I love making this woman laugh.

"I'm surprised Charming Lake even needs a police department."

"Somebody has to go door-to-door in April reminding residents to license their dogs or we'd just have dogs running around without jingling tags, sneaking up on people." I shrug. "Also, we need blue lights in the parade."

By the time we reach the highway, she's relaxed in the seat

and her coffee's almost gone, but she's being quiet. No humming along with the Christmas songs the radio station is playing. No asking questions about the scenery.

"I don't understand why we're doing this," she says abruptly, as if the words burst out of her. "I have a discretionary credit card from Mr. Wilson, and I could easily handle this online."

I'm surprised it took her this long to bring it up. "That's not the point."

"Buying everything on the list as efficiently as possible—while not wasting gas *and* both of our days, I might add—isn't the point?"

"No." The word comes out more intensely than I intended, but her thinking this day is a waste of time irks me. "Efficiency is *not* the point."

"Putting on a Christmas fair *is* the point, and we could check off a lot of tasks in the half a day—or more—we'd save if I bought the items we need online."

"Look, usually when the fire department shows up for our community, it's because somebody is having a really bad day—maybe the worst day they'll ever have. And they're not strangers. When we respond to an emergency, chances are good that somebody is a person we know and care about. We know the people whose house is on fire. We know the driver who hit a patch of ice and wrapped their car around a utility pole. We know the woman having a stroke in the market, and we know the people on their knees in tears next to the man in cardiac arrest because they know we're too late. So when my firefighters and I get a chance to be a part of a *good* day for our community—a day of joy and laughter and celebration—it is absolutely *not* a waste of our time."

As soon as I'm done talking, I realize I went too far. I overreacted because this *is* just a job for her—and not a job she sought out, but one assigned to her by her boss. I glance sideways at her, about to apologize, but the softness in her face stops me.

"I'm sorry," she says. "I have a tendency to get hung up on business and data and efficiency, and that was very thoughtless of me."

"I might have gone a little hard. It's not fair of me to expect you to have an emotional connection to a community you've been in for what…five days?"

She smiles—a real one, even—and then takes another sip of her coffee. "I'm very, very fond of Beth already."

By the time I pull into the big box store's parking lot, our cups are empty. We're caffeinated and ready to shop.

I grab a cart from the corral, and head straight for a display of funny ugly sweaters. I lift one off the rack and turn to show it to Whitney. She's several feet behind me, arms crossed and head tilted down a different aisle.

"Is there any point in telling you holiday sweaters are not on the list?" she asks. I shake my head, and I can see her struggling to keep a straight face. "Is there any point in trying to move through this store in a logical, efficient way?"

I shake my head again and point to the sweater in my hand. "You can't expect me to ignore a sweater like this."

"I didn't think so." She loses the battle and laughs. "You should get it. It's very you."

I frown and look at the sweater again. "I was thinking for you. For the Christmas fair."

"No."

"But the jingle bells are real and all the bulbs actually light up." I hit the *test me* button to show her. "It's very festive."

"I'll think about it," she says in the same way my mom used to say, 'we'll see'. Every kid—and grown man—knows that's a deferred *no*. "Let's get this list handled and we'll circle back to it after."

She's hoping I'll forget about it, but I let her have the temporary win. Whitney might be efficient, but I'm stubborn.

"Lead on, then, Ms. Forrester. Let's go forth and be efficiently merry."

She's laughing as she walks away, and I'm so entranced by the sound, I almost miss the five-dollar DVD bin.

CHAPTER
Eleven

WHITNEY

We have two carts now. Halfway through the list, I had to go back to the entrance for an empty one. Then, even though I was only gone for a few minutes, I had to hunt through the maze of aisles and shoppers to find Rob again.

The man can *not* stick to a plan.

As I watch him trying to decide if mini slingshots that fling fake reindeer poop are good toys for the older elementary-age kids—and no, they are not—I think about the fire station. It's incredibly organized and neat, though his desk is a bit of a mess. He's responsible for the lives and safety of a community he loves, and they didn't make him the chief for grins.

It's almost as if Rob takes his responsibilities so seriously that when he's off the clock, he just goes with the flow. And now he's got me going with the flow, too. While we're steadily checking things off the list, we're doing it in the most unfocused and chaotic way possible.

And I'm having so much fun. It's impossible not to enjoy

watching Rob trying on antler headbands, getting excited about the tiny fire station in the Christmas village aisle. If a toy has a button to sample the sound it makes, he pushes it.

I wander off while he's helping a boy search through the Hot Wheels cars, most of which the boy can't reach—and find myself in the doll aisle.

I check my list because one of the children asked for a very specific doll and since her mother recently underwent a major surgery, the Santa Fund is helping her acquire presents for her kids.

It takes me a few minutes to find it, but I add it to the cart, wondering if we're going to need a third one before we get out of this store. Then a doll wearing a patchwork dress catches my eye and I pick it up. I've never seen one before, but something about the simple dress and braided hair reminds me of my mom. It doesn't make sense, other than reminding me of her affinity for antique rag dolls, but it brings me straight back to the year I asked for a doll for Christmas.

I don't even remember what the doll was—some kind of fancy Barbie doll, I think—but I desperately wanted one. And I was disappointed on Christmas morning when, surrounded by discarded wrapping paper, there was no doll.

Later that evening, when I had Christmas dinner with my dad, his wife and my very young half-brothers, I'd gotten the doll. No matter how hard I try, I can't remember what the doll actually looked like. But I remember his acceptance of a thank-you kiss to the cheek and his utter disinterest in the gifts he—or maybe his wife or an assistant—had bought me.

I don't have to put any effort into recalling opening gifts with my mother. Because we didn't have a lot, she always made the unwrapping an adventure. Lots of ribbons, colorful strings. Bows. So much tape. I used to tease her about her wrapping abilities because of how much tape she used.

Looking back, I realize it slowed the morning down. It

took me longer to open my gifts, and there was so much laughter. Christmas mornings with her didn't have the kind of gifts that were under my father's austere Christmas tree, but try as I might, I can't remember my father laughing.

Dad bought me a gaming system that was the envy of my friends. I don't remember if it was an X-Box or a PlayStation. Maybe he bought me both.

Mom gave me a notebook with a pen loop, and she'd gone through the pages, leaving doodles and little messages of encouragement. That first journal held my dreams and the goals I needed to reach to make them come true. It taught me that nothing focuses my mind like pen and paper, and I still have it on my small bookshelf in my tiny apartment.

"I hate to interrupt," Rob says, making me jump. "But she's not talking to you, is she?"

"What?"

"The doll. You've been staring at her, and you were frowning and then you looked a little emotional, but then you smiled. I'm not sure if Beth put too much espresso in that coffee, or if you're having an actual conversation with that toy."

"Maybe she's the Ghost of Christmas Present."

He laughs and then gestures toward my cart. "Then you *have* to buy her."

I put the doll back on the shelf. "I don't have anybody to buy her for."

"I meant for yourself."

"We're not here to shop for ourselves."

Rob whistles nonchalantly while ever-so-slowly moving a bunch of children's mittens so they cover a Hot Wheels firetruck. I laugh and start pushing my cart away from him.

"We're almost done, Rob. Let's just focus on the list so we can get out of here. It feels like time has no meaning here and we're going to stagger outside only to find out we missed New Year's."

We finally cross almost everything off the list—there are a few items Rob concedes I'll have to order online—and head to the check-out. We bought so much stuff, it doesn't fit on the cash register belt, so I have to go get an empty cart to load the purchases into as they're bagged. From the corner of my eye, I see him push that ugly sweater through, and I let it go. I'm almost looking forward to the battle over whether or not I'll wear it to the Christmas fair.

When I see Rob pull a journal with a bright floral cover out of the second cart, though, I call his name. "That must have fallen out of the seat into the basket. That's mine, along with those socks."

He holds up the thick, fuzzy socks decorated with Christmas penguins. "These socks? Are you trying to be secretly festive, Ms. Forrester?"

"They're for my mom. Put those two things aside and I'll pay for them after."

"They won't even put a dent in the bottom line."

"I'm not misappropriating funds from the Santa Fund, Chief Byrne," I say with exaggerated snippiness, and he chuckles as he sets my items back in the seat.

He ducks into the men's room while I pay for my purchases, and I'm standing near the exit with two full carts when he emerges.

"There must be somebody wrapping gifts for a fundraiser somewhere around here," I say. "If we can find one with multiple wrapping stations, it'll still take a while, but maybe not *forever*."

"No need. My family wraps the gifts."

"*All* of them?"

"No, we wrap the ones for the good kids in Christmas paper and the naughty ones get their gifts in brown paper bags." He's already pushing one cart toward the door, but the cheeky grin he gives me over his shoulder makes me laugh as I follow him.

I think I've laughed more today than I have all year, and as I hand the bags up to Rob to stow in the bed of his truck, I realize this has been one of the best days I've had in a long time. I'm not sure why doing a massive shopping trip with a guy who moves through the store like a mouse looking for peanut butter in a maze was fun, but I can't deny that it was.

Once we finally reach the last bag, I return the empty carts while he rolls down the black leather thing that covers the bed of the truck and will keep bags from blowing out, raining toys and candy all over the cars behind us on the highway.

"I think it's time for a burger and fries," he says once we're in the truck. "Want to hit the diner for lunch?"

I shouldn't. What I *should* do is go back to the inn, make a sandwich, and isolate myself in my room. I need to dance it out. Reset myself, and shake off the uncharacteristically relaxed vibe so I can focus on the next task on the list.

"Let me show you the magic that is vinegar on your fries," he adds when I don't answer right away. After shifting the truck into gear, he gives me one more grin. "It'll change your life."

I actually kind of like the version of me I am with Rob, so what the hell, right? "Okay, Rob. Change my life."

CHAPTER
Twelve

ROB

"You can't just dump the vinegar on top." Usually I wouldn't make such a production out of getting my fries ready to eat, but trying to pretend to take me seriously when she thinks I'm being ridiculous is my favorite of Whitney's expressions —the way the effort not to smile plays with her mouth is sexy as hell—and I don't want to stop.

"No dumping vinegar," she says, nodding. Then she pulls her notebook out of her bag and opens it to a fresh page. After clicking her pen, she looks at me expectantly.

"Wait. You're not actually going to write that down, are you?"

She laughs and closes the book. "No."

"I can never be sure with you because getting stuff done is your superpower and I'm pretty sure that notebook is your magical artifact."

"Magical artifact?"

"Yeah, you know. Like a hammer that smashes everything, or a lasso that forces people to tell the truth." She laughs again, and I raise the salt shaker, needing to get us back on track before the fries get cold. "A light sprinkle of salt. Then a sprinkle of white vinegar across the top."

"I definitely should be writing this down," she says as I demonstrate.

"You're just mocking me now." I use my fingers to toss the fries without letting any fall off the plate. "Mix it up a bit. Then another dash of salt and a final sprinkling of vinegar. It's all in the layering."

I hold the fry out to her, stretching my arm across the table so she can smell the vinegar. I'm wondering if that was a mistake—I happen to like that smell, but I know from Lyla's reaction if she stops by when I'm cleaning that not everybody does—when Whitney bites off the end of the fry.

The jolt of desire hits me like pure electricity running through my veins, and I imagine her taking another bite so her lips meet my fingers. Then, because my mind is a horny trickster, I get an image of her slowly sucking the salt from my fingers and, dammit, my jeans are pretty uncomfortable all of a sudden.

Before I can figure out what to do with the fry, she snatches the remaining piece from me and pops it in her mouth. Luckily, she seems oblivious to my discomfort and the fact my face is probably as red as the vinyl seats.

"That's delicious," she says, sprinkling vinegar over her own fries. "It seems wrong that something can be used as a household cleaning product and also make french fries delicious, doesn't it?"

I clear my throat in the hope my voice won't come out sounding like a man who just pictured her sucking said cleaning product-slash-condiment off my fingers. "But it works."

The conversation dies off as we dive into our lunches, taking the edge off the kind of appetite a morning of shopping works up. But as I'm working my way through my burger, I wonder just how bad I should be feeling about my attraction to the woman sitting across from me.

Sure, there's the fact she works for my brother-in-law and, since he assigned her to help me, she's kind of working for me, as well. Not officially, but I know she feels as if her work on the Christmas fair will influence Donovan's opinion of her, so that's kind of messy.

But also, I don't know a lot about her personal life. Just because she's here in Charming Lake with the holiday right around the corner doesn't mean there's nobody waiting at home for her. It just means she put her job first, and that wouldn't be out of character for Whitney.

"Do you have a significant other waiting for you back home?" I ask because I can't find a more graceful way to ease into the topic. "Being in Charming Lake for two weeks in December is a big ask on Donovan's part."

Whitney doesn't look offended by the question, thankfully. "There's nobody right now. And before you think it's because I'm focused on my career, it's more that I've been comfortable with my life and haven't really made an effort."

"Be honest. There was a guy, and he didn't put the deli meats in the deli meats drawer, right?"

She laughs so loudly, several other diners turn to look. "He alphabetized my spices, thank you very much."

"Huh. I would have guessed you were into that sort of thing."

"I organize my spices according to how frequently I use them, so the ones I use the most are easily at hand. It's about efficiency, not just organization for organization's sake." She takes a sip of the ice water she ordered with her coffee. "What about you? I haven't heard you mention a significant other."

"Nope."

She tilts her head, looking thoughtful. "So what do the good people of Charming Lake know that I don't? Because— on the surface, at least—you're attractive and funny, and you have a stable job. I'm surprised you don't need one of those deli number dispensers."

That's strangely flattering, I guess. "You have to remember I've known most of the women around here for my entire life, so a lot of them had taken a number before we graduated from high school, so to speak. And it's not easy finding a woman who loves this town as much as I do, and who wants to spend her entire life here. Also, one who'll consider the entire community part of our family."

"Including that guy who just walks up one side of the main street and down the other, glaring at people?"

"Including that guy. Maybe *especially* that guy. You see a grumpy old man walking around being grumpy. I see a retired lawyer who lost his wife in the car accident that left him in chronic pain. Clifford walks because he says the alternative is sitting around, doing nothing but waiting to join his wife. The glaring is actually squinting from the pain, and the man has given enough free legal advice during those walks to buy a private island if he charged for it. Or at least a yacht, maybe. I don't actually know how much a private island costs. I should ask Donovan."

"He doesn't own any islands." She leans forward, her expression thoughtful. "Don't you find it a little claustrophobic, knowing the life story of every person around you? And they know yours, and everybody's all up in your business all the time?"

"Sometimes," I admit. "But I think I'd find it even more claustrophobic being surrounded by a sea of strangers, with nobody up in my business at all."

"I guess I can see that. I'll be sure to smile at Clifford from now on, instead of glaring back at him."

"Now Shane, the tall guy with the fringed suede coat you can't miss, on the other hand—if you see him walking around and he glares at you, it's because he's truly miserable and hateful. He can't work up the ambition to actually go live alone in a remote, off-the-grid cabin in the woods somewhere, so I think he's actually trying to will us all to disappear."

"Good to know."

When she pulls her wallet out of her bag, I shake my head. "We're on official Santa Fund business. And before you give me hell about the appropriate use of the money, you'll notice we didn't get a bill. Barb's got us covered today."

"That's kind of her. I'm leaving a tip, though." She puts the cash on the table and drinks the last of her coffee, which is my signal it's time to go.

I wouldn't have minded staying a few more hours. Maybe we could have looped right into supper. "When I drop you off, I'll put all of this in the inn's garage so it's in one place."

She nods. "Good. That'll give me the opportunity to separate gifts from prizes and so on, since *somebody* just threw everything on the belt in random order, so it all got bagged together."

It's so sexy when she tries to scold me, but the curve of her lips gives away the fact she actually finds me charming. "You're not going to leave me much to do."

"Literally my job," she says, and then she laughs for a second before pulling out her notebook and flipping to a page filled with very neat printing. "Do you have stuff scheduled for tomorrow that I should know about, or should I just drink extra coffee and hope for the best?"

"I think we'll drive around and get people to sign those participation forms in person, so at least the parade line-up will be checked off. And we need to figure out who has the Santa suit."

"You don't know who has it? Is this like a Sisterhood of the Traveling Santa Suit situation?"

"Well, you know how it goes. It went to one person for cleaning. And then somebody else was going to stitch up some loose seams. But the fake fur trim was looking raggedy, so...somebody has it, though."

"And you don't just buy a new suit because…"

"I think the current suit is older than me, and they don't make them like that anymore."

She shakes her head and slides out of the booth. "Okay, so tomorrow is paperwork and a Santa suit scavenger hunt. I'll bring the coffee."

CHAPTER
Thirteen

WHITNEY

I open my notebook to the page my pen is clipped on and make a checkmark next to the bakery's name to indicate we have their signed paperwork and that task is complete. Everybody who signed up is now parade official.

Now we're on our way to the last known location of the wayward Santa suit.

Through the corner of my eye, I see him watching me stow the notebook back in my bag. "You've got the laptop and the tablet and your phone and the watch, and you seem like a very plugged-in kind of person. And yet you use a notebook instead of a digital notepad app."

"I learned a long time ago, when my mom bought me a notebook for Christmas, that I think best with pen and paper. Brainstorming and just letting thoughts come and stuff like that. You know I love my spreadsheets and lists and tables, but those are boxes the info goes into. If you start with those, the creative part of your mind is trying to fit those boxes. When you have an empty page in front of you, you can do anything you want and then worry about slotting it into the proper boxes later."

"So what you're saying is that your mom got you a Christmas present that changed your life?"

"Maybe not as life-changing as vinegar on fries, but yeah." I don't really want to talk about my mom. Something about this town has me thinking about her a lot, and I keep remembering the sad resignation in her voice when I told her I'd be busy at Christmas, catching up in the office after being stuck in New Hampshire for two weeks.

So I change the subject. "Do you drive this vehicle in the parade?"

"I should. My predecessor drove his with the lights on and one of the guys drove the firetruck. But my deputy chief owns an excavation business and he likes to drive his own truck, pulling a backhoe they decorate with lights and stuff. Another one of the guys owns the antique tractor that pulls the church's float, and he won't let anybody else drive it. The others have small kids and they gear up and walk along the parade route with their families, interacting and stuff. So I drive the firetruck."

"That's way cooler than an SUV, anyway. Anybody can drive one of those."

"That's what I think, too." He turns right onto a poorly paved road, and I'm thankful I wasn't sipping my coffee at the time or I would have worn it. "You should ride in the firetruck with me for the parade."

I laugh until I realize he's serious. "I'm not riding in the firetruck with you. What if a problem pops up I need to address?"

"You found Donovan refills for his favorite pen from across the ocean. If something comes up at the fair, I'm confident you can fix it from the middle of Main Street. We go pretty slow, so you could even jump out if you had to. Just tuck and roll." He takes a left onto a dirt road. "Actually, you're so good at your job, I don't think there will be any problems at all."

His praise warms my cheeks, and I look out my window so he can't see it. "What happens if there's an actual emergency during the parade? Do you just turn the sirens on and make everybody scatter?"

He laughs as though he's imagining doing just that. "We report as out of service during the parade, and our mutual aid partners from nearby towns handle anything that comes up. We do the same for them. Most of Charming Lake is *at* the parade, though, so it's rare to have an emergency pop up. We had a fall on the ice once, but mostly we just yell at the people on the floats for not dressing warmly enough."

"It's like Halloween. Nobody wants to cover their costumes."

"Nobody likes getting frostbite, either. But I think Charming Lake's only had one fire on the day of the Christmas fair during my lifetime. An older couple was rushing so they wouldn't miss the parade and each thought the other blew their scented candle out. Their cat and some Christmas decorations were involved somehow—I was in high school still, so I don't know all the details—but FD was able to save everything. Things got a little soggy, of course, but it could have been worse."

After flipping on his turn signal, Rob pulls into a driveway and throws the SUV in park. "I'll be right back."

"I don't believe you."

"I know I said that before, but George wanted to give me hell about the increase in the fuel budget for the fire department and he wasn't really understanding that if he's paying more at the pump, maybe we are, too."

"And the time before that?"

"Oh, Kath wanted me to have some pie."

I reach over and slap his arm. "You had pie while I sat in your truck?"

"No!" He makes a big show out of rubbing his arm, even though my nails barely grazed him. "She wanted me to have some cherry pie, but I declined and it can take a while to keep persistently declining until the other person gives up."

I narrow my eyes. "Is offering you some cherry pie a euphemism? I've heard fire fighters get a lot of calls from lonely damsels who aren't in the 9-1-1 kind of distress."

"No, it was literal pie, but—between you and me—Kath might be the worst baker in the entire state. Possibly in New England." He nudges me with his elbow, grinning. "Why? Are you jealous?"

I snort and turn my head away, looking out my window and folding my arms as if that idea is too ludicrous to consider. It's true, actually, but I'm not about to give him the satisfaction.

A blast of cold air followed by the closing of his door tells me he's gone, and I turn the radio up so I can sing along with the Christmas songs in peace.

He's only gone ten minutes this time, and he emerges with a large plastic tote. More cold air swirls in from the back when he opens the lift gate and shoves it into the back of the SUV.

"Sorry," he says once he's back in the driver's seat. "It wasn't enough to give me the damn suit. I had to hear all about how it's been taking up room in her attic but that she doesn't really mind because her grandmother made it and somehow she saw that as a segue to talking about what a jerk her grandfather was and how nobody was sad when he *accidentally* killed himself falling off the ladder while cleaning the gutters."

"Why do I get the impression there are implied air quotes around *accidentally*?"

He gives me a raised eyebrow look before backing out of the driveway. "Well, it was before my time, of course, but there was some question about trajectory—like where he would have landed if he fell versus where he might have landed if somebody reached out a second-story window and gave the ladder a good push—but the police chief at the time didn't want to prolong his newly widowed sister's grief by digging too deep."

"Oh. *Wow*."

"Let's just say the people who were in charge of determining his cause of death were also people privy to how many times his wife went to the ER due to being clumsy."

"Well, that story was certainly worth sitting in the car for," I say. "What's next?"

"Next, you have to help me get the suit on so we can inspect it because everybody I talked to thinks somebody else fixed it and we can't have it coming apart on the big day. And with a storm coming, we'll lose some of our time to get things done."

"There's a storm coming?" When he glances over at me, frowning, I know he's going to make a crack about me not being on top of the weather. "My app is set to the weather at Mr. Wilson's location, so I'll be notified of any potential issues with his schedule."

"Well, there's a bunch of snow coming *our* way. Penny will know it's coming and have everything needed for food and supplies, but don't plan on going out after noon tomorrow and probably through Sunday."

I look out my window, already dreading not being able to get to the General Store. The inn has coffee, of course, but it's not as good as Beth's. Of course, nobody delivers. "And just when I was starting to like this town."

CHAPTER
Fourteen

ROB

"I feel ridiculous."

Whitney laughs at me, her hands on her hips. "You're wearing a Santa costume that's decades old and at least ten sizes too big. I can't believe your expectation was anything *but* looking ridiculous."

"It's not *supposed* to fit because there has to be room for padding. It won't look ridiculous on Jerry."

"Wait. Jerry, the guy who signed the waiver form for the hardware store?"

"Yes. That Jerry."

"Is he even capable of holding up the amount of padding he'll need to fill this out?"

I nod, making the bell on the Santa hat's pompom ring. "He's thin, but he's very strong. Wiry as hell, according to him. But anyway, is there anything else in the tote? Where's the belt?"

"There's no point in putting on the belt," she mutters as

she digs through the plastic tote. "We'd have to wrap it around you four times. There's a—"

Her mouth snaps shut when she pulls out a short, green minidress with candy cane buttons. I'd forgotten the sexy elf dress was still around.

She turns to face me, holding up the dress. "I am *not* wearing this."

I try not to picture her wearing it because it feels wrong to have an erection while dressed as Santa. "Oh, come on. Every Santa needs an elf, Whitney."

"No."

I sigh dramatically. "Fine, but if you're not going to be an elf, then you have to wear the sweater."

She's fighting to keep her expression blank while avoiding direct eye contact. "What sweater?"

"You know I bought that ugly Christmas sweater for you. You do *not* overlook details, Ms. Forrester."

"I prefer pretending it doesn't exist."

"If you don't wear the sweater for the fair as one of the official organizers, then I bought it for no reason." I shrug, holding up my hands. "That means you'll be aiding and abetting me in my misappropriation of Santa Fund money."

"Fine, Rob. I'll wear the ugly sweater." She tosses the elf dress aside and pulls a black belt with a huge silver buckle out of the tote. "I own shirts longer than that dress. Hell, I think there's more fabric in this belt."

"Full disclosure—that elf costume was retired at least thirty years ago because one, it's undeniably inappropriate. But also, it's not exactly warm. We keep it, though, because they were made as a set."

"So you tricked me into agreeing to wear that sweater?"

"I can't hear you with this Santa hat sliding down over my ears. Jerry must have a bigger head than I do."

"That seems unlikely." But she's smiling when she says it,

so I know she's not mad about the sweater. "Okay, let's look and see if you're coming unraveled anywhere."

It doesn't take long to realize I've made a mistake. Making an examination of the Santa suit into a fun game of dress-up with Whitney had sounded fun. But I seriously underestimated how much havoc her being so close to me would wreak on my senses.

Because the suit is baggy, she isn't actually running her hands over my body as she checks each seam. Instead, it's all tantalizing hints of contact and the teasing pressure of her touch through the thick fabric.

Whitney checks all the seams in the jacket, seemingly oblivious to the fact she's slowly killing me.

It's my own fault. I could have done this by myself, by taking the suit out of the tote and hanging it up to air out before the parade. It would have been simple enough to look it over on a hanger. But I wanted to spend as much time as I could with Whitney—best accomplished by stretching out the fair preparations—so I brought this torture down on myself.

She's getting it done with her usual brisk efficiency until she crouches to check the seam down the outside of my right leg. My instinct is to step away, but I'm afraid she'll fall over.

Luckily, she stands and gives a hard shake of her head. Her cheeks are flushed and she's not meeting my gaze, so maybe she's not as unaffected by the close contact as I thought.

"You don't actually have to be wearing the suit for me to do this," she says. "I'll check the pants after you take them off."

Since it feels as if the temperature in the room has risen about twenty degrees in the last few minutes, it'll be a relief to get out of the heavy costume.

Unfortunately, that's easier said than done. "Whitney, the zipper's stuck."

"Don't force it! We don't want to rip the coat this close to the parade." She pushes my hands away. "Let me see it."

Whitney fiddles with the zipper while I stare at a spot on the wall over the top of her head and try not to smell her hair. She's so intent on the zipper, I don't think she realizes a person would be hard-pressed to slide a piece of cardboard between our bodies.

I realize it, though. It's taking every ounce of self-control I can muster to keep my dick from popping up and joining the conversation. I'm afraid we're close enough so she'd be able to feel it.

"Whoever cleaned and fluffed the fake fur trim did such a good job it's all caught up in the zipper," she tells me. "You need to sit down so I can see it better."

I'm relieved for the all of thirty seconds it takes for her to step away and for me to sit in a chair. Then she's standing between my knees and the hint of cleavage in the vee of her blouse is the only thing in my line of vision.

Rob Byrne, do NOT put your hands on her waist.

Along with using my sternest inner voice on myself, I ball my hands into fists. She's only this close to me because she's trying to help me, and I can't take advantage of that by putting my hands on her.

Pressing the palms of my hands flat on the tops of my thighs, I close my eyes and try to breathe normally. It's not easy, and I hope I don't pass out. That would be awkward to explain to her, plus there's the possibility Whitney panics and calls 9-1-1. That would certainly be a mess.

"I think I've got it," she mutters. "But I'll have to work out a way to keep the fluff out of the zipper or it's going to keep happening. Okay, stand up."

I'm launched into yet another cycle of relief followed by *oh no, this is worse* because Whitney's pushing the coat off of my shoulders and, in guiding the heavy fabric, she has her arms around me.

I know the exact second Whitney realizes the position we're in—her arms capturing me while her breasts press against my chest—because she freezes. The heavy coat slides down my arms and thuds to the ground, and now my arms are free.

She doesn't back up.

Her head tips back until I'm looking into her eyes. Then my gaze drops to her lips, which are slightly parted.

When her hands rest on my upper arms, the contact is like an electric current, energizing my body and making my arms move. In the space of a heartbeat, my hands are on her waist.

I don't know which of us moves first, but our mouths meet and I'm kissing her like a man who's waited his entire life to kiss the woman in his arms.

It hasn't even been a week, actually, but it certainly *feels* as if I've been waiting my entire life.

Whitney's hands move up my arms and over my shoulders to cup the back of my neck. One of my arms wraps around her waist, holding her tight against me, while I slide my other hand up her back.

She moans, her body arching against mine. The sound inflames me and I shift my head, deepening the kiss.

The movement causes the hat to shift on my head and the dangling bell jingles. Suddenly, she's giggling against my mouth and then we're both laughing, still tangled in each other's arms.

"I'm kissing Santa Claus." Whitney says, swiping at the bell dangling near my cheek. "This is so wrong."

"Oh, you're definitely on the naughty list."

I'm about to toss the hat in the corner and resume kissing her when we hear the distinctive sound of boots coming up the old wooden stairs. Whitney moves away, reaching down to snatch the coat off the floor.

"Hey, Chief, I picked up some—" Tim lifts his head and sees Whitney. "Sorry. I didn't realize you had company."

"This is Whitney Forrester. She's helping out with the Christmas fair this year. Whitney, this is Lieutenant Tim Johnson, the guy who holds everything together with me."

"Sure," Tim says, reaching out to shake Whitney's hand. "You work for Donovan, right?"

"I do. It's nice to meet you, Tim."

My lieutenant just met Whitney for the first time, so hopefully he won't notice the slight tremor in her voice. And maybe he can't see the way her neck and cheeks are a little rosier than usual. Oh, and the way her lips look as if she's just been thoroughly kissed.

"I stopped by to help you get ready for the storm," Tim says. "But I can come back later if you're busy."

"No," Whitney says, far too quickly for my liking. "We're done here. I'll take the suit back to the inn and finish getting it ready for the parade. I have some other work I need to get done, too."

I don't want her to leave like this, but she's backed me into a corner. There's no way I can argue with that without cluing Tim into the fact that, yes, he'd interrupted a lot more than a business meeting.

Clearly flustered, Whitney shoves all the parts of the Santa suit back into the tote and snaps the lid on. Before I can step forward, Tim lifts it off the floor.

"I'll carry this for you," he says, and Whitney smiles before making sure she has her bag and her keys.

"I hope the storm goes easy on you," she says to me, though she's looking at my mouth and not my eyes. "I'll be hanging around the inn once it starts because I don't mind driving, but my winter-weather skills are a bit rusty."

I want to say something—*anything*—about the kiss, but I can't because Tim's standing there holding a heavy tote, waiting for Whitney. I could take it from him and walk her out, but I'm not sure what I'd say and she looks eager to exit the situation.

"If you need anything, just call or shoot me a text."

"I'll see you after the weather clears, I guess." And then she's walking down the stairs with Tim behind her.

It'll probably be Monday before I see Whitney again, and it shouldn't feel like forever. I haven't even known her that long. But the idea of a couple of days passing without seeing her—especially with the memory of our kiss lingering unresolved—is enough to put a serious damper on my mood.

But I know my community well enough to know some of them think having four-wheel-drive means they're impervious to slick roads, so I need to concentrate more on the coming storm and less on kissing Whitney.

CHAPTER
Fifteen

WHITNEY

With the snow forecast to start falling around lunchtime, I decide it's safe to run a couple of errands in the morning. My first stop will be the Wilson house, so I can make sure Natalie has anything and everything she needs to weather the storm.

My second stop will be the General Store for the last scrumptious coffee I'll have until Monday morning at the earliest.

After pulling into the driveway of the Wilson home, I get out and walk to the front door. Then I hesitate because what if one or both of them is napping? Do three-year-olds nap? I have no idea. But I'm guessing pregnant women do, if they get the chance.

I'm debating whether I should text her that I'm outside when the door opens.

"Oh," I say, so startled I almost drop my phone. "I'm sorry."

She tilts her head, looking confused, but not like a pregnant mother of a toddler whose sleep was interrupted. "For what?"

"For disturbing you. Also, for standing awkwardly on your step because I realized too late I might wake you or Sam if I rang the doorbell."

She laughs and steps back, gesturing for me to come inside. "I'm alone at the moment, actually. My mother told me I should nap, but I don't want to waste the peace and quiet by sleeping through it. Have a seat."

I sit on the edge of the chair she points to, but I'm not staying long. "I'll let you get back to your peace and quiet. I just wanted to make sure you have everything you need before the storm."

"My mother and my sisters are all over this, I promise. Between Donovan traveling for business and this Christmas fair, I think you've got your hands full."

I do have a lot on my plate, but I know my boss—nothing is as important as his family. "There's no good way to phrase this, so I guess I'll just say it outright. Sometimes there are things you don't want to bother the people you love with, but it's different if a person is being paid to make sure you have everything you need."

Natalie laughs, but it's a warm and friendly sound. "You're paid to make sure Donovan Wilson, CEO, has every-thing *he* needs."

"And Donovan Wilson, CEO, needs a happy and healthy family."

Natalie sighs and rubs her hand over the top of her very large baby bump. She looks content, so I'm not alarmed, but it makes me nervous. "I have everything I need to get through the storm. My parents and Sam are picking up some last-minute things, and they'll be staying with us here until the roads are clear after the storm."

I feel a little ridiculous now. The Byrnes, with their roots in Charming Lake and ever-expanding family tree, have a lot more experience with winter storms and pregnancies than I do. I'm probably the *least* qualified person to offer help in this situation.

"And if my cell phone number comes up on Rob's phone," Natalie continues, "he'd probably be halfway here before it rang a second time."

Laughing, I imagine Rob's reaction to a call from his sister during a storm. "Usually I'd think you were exaggerating, but I'm not sure you're wrong about that."

"How's that going, by the way? Working with Rob, I mean."

Working with Rob is turning my life upside down because he's pretty much the opposite of everything I want in my life, but I can't stop thinking about him. Oh, and we kissed and I desperately want to kiss him again and it's hard to do my job when I just want to relive it over and over. "It's good. We're getting a lot done and, even with this storm, we're on track for a fabulous Charming Lake Christmas Fair."

"I heard you had a fun lunch at the diner. Lots of laughing, which is good because I was afraid your management styles would clash."

"Oh, they clash. But we also complement each other." I'm going to pretend I didn't hear the part about the diner.

That damn french fry. The idea somebody saw me eat the fry out of Rob's hand and reported back to Natalie makes me want to cover my face with my hands, but I keep them clenched in my lap.

I still don't know what possessed me to do it. We were having fun and it was playful. But the look in Rob's eyes after was so intensely hot I almost choked on the salt-and-vinegar-coated potato. That man was thinking filthy thoughts, and if we hadn't been sitting in the diner, I might have coaxed him into sharing them with me.

None of this was information I wanted Natalie to have. Or her husband.

"I guess I'll head back to the inn before the snow starts," I say, getting to my feet. "Are you sure you don't want me to do anything for you before I go?"

"I'm sure. My parents and Sam will be back any minute. The best thing you can do for me is get back to the inn and stay there. Donovan's said many times he's not sure what he would do without you. And Rob says he might have given up on the whole fair thing if he didn't have you, so we've got to keep *you* safe."

My skin warms with pleasure at the compliments, and after saying goodbye, I think about Natalie's words while driving to the General Store.

I should be dwelling on the endorsement from my boss. Rob was talking about a one-day celebration that, no matter what he said, he wouldn't give up on. Donovan owns the company I work for and his opinion of me directly impacts my career.

But, just like when I'm alone in bed or just alone in general, it's thoughts of Rob that keep me company as I head to the General Store.

CHAPTER
Sixteen

ROB

"We've got this under control if you want to check on your family, Chief."

I look at Kevin—the youngest member of the crew—over the crumpled hood of the car that got punted into a tree by an SUV that lost traction. No injuries, thankfully, but now we're standing around waiting for the tow truck.

"What do you mean?" I ask. "I don't think any of my family's there right now."

"Oh. You keep staring at the inn, so I figured they were."

I don't want to tell him I thought I caught a glimpse of Whitney through a window earlier, and I'm hoping for another. Of course, it was just my luck that, after countless hours of trying not to think about her, we got called to a minor accident right in front of the inn.

Unfortunately, the exchange catches Tim's attention, and my lieutenant gives me a knowing look. "No reason you can't pop in and make sure that city girl's got everything she needs."

The phrase *city girl* grates on my nerves, and I give him a hard stare meant to let him know the innuendo was neither lost on me nor appreciated.

The worst part is how I'd been thinking about just that. There was no reason I couldn't take a minute and cross the street to check on Whitney. She's probably not used to being stuck in a strange house by a snowstorm, and she's been helping me with the Christmas fair. Running over to see how she's doing would be a neighborly thing to do.

But now that Tim opened his mouth, going out of my way to see Whitney would open the door to a lot more teasing and innuendo.

Approaching blue lights save me from having to make a decision. The SUV with the Charming Lake Police Department logo on the door finds a safe place to pull off, and I'm not surprised when Officer Jason Carlisle steps out.

Or Jace, as we call him. Or used to, for some of us.

It's tough, when you grow up friends with a guy and then you have to adjust to him dating your sister. It gets even worse when he cheats and breaks her heart.

So here we are, in a weird place where we were once almost as close as brothers, and now we barely speak. We're thrown together often because Charming Lake is a small town. He's with the PD and I'm with the FD and our paths cross. There's always an instant where I want to greet him like the lifelong friend he was, and then I remember.

He crossed over the line and, as far as the Byrne family is concerned, there's no crossing back.

"Good of you to show up," I tell him in a flat voice. "I have the contact info for the drivers. It was all very amicable and clear-cut, and the driver of the mostly unscathed SUV gave the guy driving the car a ride home, so you can get in touch with them for your report."

A familiar shadow crosses his expression at my curt tone. The man is a walking billboard for regret, but we take our lead from Erin and until she's forgiven him, this is where we are.

"The tow truck's almost here," he says, mirroring my tone as he nods toward the flashing yellow lights in the distance. "I'll go stop traffic so people don't come around the corner and slide into him while he's loading."

Loading up a vehicle in bad weather is something we're pretty good at, so before long the tow truck, the police cruiser and the fire truck are heading out.

With Tim gone, I could probably stop in at the inn for a few minutes without attracting his ridicule. I've been standing outside in the snow for quite a while, so begging for a hot coffee from Penny wouldn't raise any eyebrows. And if I happen to see Whitney…

A familiar squawk from my radio ruins that plan, and a moment later, I'm buckling my seatbelt to rescue yet another driver who doesn't grasp that two-wheel-drive versus four-wheel-drive is a moot point if the road is coated with ice.

As I turn my SUV around, though, I can't help glancing at the inn one more time. The downstairs windows are empty, but I glance up and see Whitney smiling down at me from the window in her room.

I smile back, lifting my hand in greeting. She presses her hand against the glass as I drive away, humming a jaunty Christmas song under my breath.

Tomorrow, I think. The roads will be clear and I'll get to see Whitney again.

CHAPTER
Seventeen

WHITNEY

Once the Charming Lake Fire Department has cleared the scene in front of the inn and driven away, there isn't much to keep me occupied.

The boss doesn't need anything from me, nor does his wife. The office is running smoothly. There really isn't anything I can check off the Christmas fair list while trapped inside. Information and tasks can only be organized so much without doing the actual work.

With nothing to keep my brain too occupied to replay kissing Rob over and over, I wander toward the kitchen, looking for distraction. The closer I get, the more delicious the house smells, so at the very least, I might score a yummy snack.

Penny looks up from the process of dropping cookie dough onto a sheet pan, but I can see a rack of freshly baked cookies cooling behind her.

"Is there something you need, Miss Forrester?"

"No, thank you. I'm just going to grab a coffee to fuel my aimless wanderings."

"I brewed a pot not too long ago, and I've only had one cup from it. It's still pretty fresh." She sighs and looks over the baking supplies strewn over the kitchen island. "I'm just trying to get these cookies baked before I head home to Maine for the holidays on Thursday morning."

My brain is so muddled by the aroma of freshly baked cookies and promise of coffee, it takes a minute for the rest of what she said to sink in. "You're leaving Thursday?"

"Christmas is a big deal for my family. And the inn closes for the holidays, reopening the weekend after New Year's, so it's a lovely paid vacation for me."

Usually I'd be focused on the fiscal impact of not only closing down a business for weeks, but paying employees for the time off. Right now, though, I'm more focused on the fact *the inn is closing*.

"Mr. Wilson didn't tell me the inn is closing." He also didn't tell me where I'm supposed to sleep once it does. Am I supposed to go back to the city earlier than I thought? I assumed I'd stay through the fair itself, at least.

"Closing to *guests*," she says quickly. "The family stays here, so you won't be rattling around this big house alone."

"The family stays here," I repeat, and I'm not sure if that makes it better or worse. "All of them?"

Penny laughs. "No, not all of them. And they come and go. Nana Jo stays in the room on this floor because getting ready for the Christmas fair means the entire family will come through at some point. The grandkids stay. And Donovan's mom and stepmom are coming this year, so they'll get one of the rooms. I'm not sure how many are planning to sleep here, but it'll all get figured out."

I barely keep myself from asking if Rob stays at the house. I'm guessing not, since it sounds like the place will be full and, whether he's at his home or the fire station, it's close enough to pop by.

Even though I enjoy his company—and there's an understatement if I've ever heard one—it's probably for the best. I have a hard enough time forcing myself to sleep instead of imagining all the things I'd like to do with Rob Byrne without him being under the same roof.

After preparing myself a large mug of coffee, I lean my hip against the counter and watch Penny slide the cookie sheet into the oven. After setting the timer, she takes a long sip of her own coffee.

"You said you're heading *home* to Maine," I say. "Are you not from here, then?"

"No, I'm not." She chuckles. "It's funny that I said going *home* to Maine when I've lived in Charming Lake for almost twenty years. My husband took a teaching job at the elementary school, so we moved here. The marriage ended, but my love for this town didn't, so here I am."

The phone rings—the inn's business line—before I can ask her any more questions, so when she waves for me to help myself to the cooling rack, I top off my coffee, take two cookies and leave her to the phone call.

Rather than going back upstairs to my room, I head for the cozy sitting room. The gas fireplace is on, the flames low, and I curl up at one end of the comfortable sofa. There are coasters on the antique wooden coffee table, and I set my mug down while I nibble at the cookies and skim through my email.

As expected, there isn't much going on in my email account this close to Christmas. Even though it's still two weeks away, any sense of urgency has given way to the inevitable *after the holidays*.

I open the Facebook app and scroll through the various posts from my family and friends. I rarely say anything myself, but I enjoy seeing photos.

At this time of year, most of them have to do with the

upcoming holiday, of course. And by some weird twist of algorithmic fate, my stepmother's decorated living room photo is followed immediately by my mother's.

My father's house has been decorated in the same style for as long as I remember—elegant, with a lot of green boughs and white lights. The few ornaments are glass and perfectly matched. The decor isn't exactly warm and festive, but it certainly photographs well.

My mother's house, though? It looks like somebody spent ten years buying Christmas decorations at rummage sales, put them in a big bin, shook it, and then tossed it around her living room. If there was a theme, it would be *raggedy Christmas decorations her daughter made in school*, and no matter how many times I see her holiday photos come up year after year, they always make me smile.

I almost choke on the sip of coffee I just took when my phone buzzes in my hand with a text message from Rob.

Leave some cookies for the family.

I laugh out loud, setting my coffee down. Then I glance over my shoulder to see if I've attracted Penny's attention. When she doesn't come in from the kitchen, I snuggle deeper into the couch.

I know this is a small town, but you've already heard I raided the stash Penny's making to hold you all over?

Just a lucky guess.

Mr. Wilson neglected to tell me the innkeeper would be leaving and the entire Byrne family would be moving in.

Not all of us.

I type out a somewhat flirty comment, telling him that was too bad, and then I delete it. And then I can't think of another response and then the panic sets in because if he was watching his screen, he'll have seen the dots and then the pause. He'll know I was going to say something and thought better of it.

I'll leave a few cookies for you, I finally type.

The storm's finally winding down, so the roads should be clear in the morning. We've got a lot to do, so if you're not comfortable driving, let me know and I can pick you up.

I'll let you know in the morning. Either way, the first thing on the list is visiting the General Store for coffee.

I like that plan. See you tomorrow.

When I find myself clutching my phone to my chest like a middle school girl who just got a phone call from her crush, I force myself to open my email app again to refocus myself.

Maybe I should switch to decaf.

CHAPTER
Eighteen

ROB

The roads are clear enough for Whitney to drive herself in by late morning, and I'm not surprised when she shows up with a coffee for each of us.

I spent a decent chunk of time last night lying in my bed, wondering what the vibe between us will be. Will it be awkward? Will I get to kiss her hello, or is she going to pretend it never happened?

It's no wonder I can barely think over the sound of my heartbeat as she crosses the equipment bay toward me.

"Today is not only Monday, but half the day is gone, and the Christmas fair is Saturday," she says, handing me one of the cups. "We need to get to work."

She doesn't meet my eyes when she says it, so I assume that's her way of answering my unasked question of where we go from here.

I guess we're pretending the kiss didn't happen. Okay, then.

"We should go scope out the main street," I tell her. It's

going to be nice today and tomorrow, but we're in for a cold snap Wednesday and Thursday nights."

"A cold snap? Has it not *been* cold this whole time, including so cold we got dumped on by snow?"

I chuckle at her indignant expression. "By cold snap, I mean dipping down into temps that will turn any cute, fluffy piles of snow into frozen boulders. We need to look at the map we sketched out and make sure that anywhere we plan to set up activities gets cleared out before it freezes."

"This may come as a shock to you, but I'm not great with a snow shovel."

"So what I'm hearing is that you need practice." When her eyes widen, I laugh. "We'll make a list of trouble spots and I'll get it to town hall so the Public Works guys can get on it."

"I have the map on my phone."

"And while we're out driving around, we should stop by my place and grab the paint for the sleigh."

She sighs, looking disappointed in me, but not surprised. "We have to paint a sleigh? I didn't see that noted anywhere, and you haven't mentioned it."

"When I dropped it in the inn's event barn to store it because the person who *was* storing it bought himself a project car and needed the space, I noticed it was looking a bit shabby, but I didn't write it down."

"Wouldn't it make more sense to park your SUV outside and put the sleigh in here, since you're always here?"

"It makes perfect sense until somebody calls 9-1-1 and it takes me ten minutes to scrape the snow and ice off my windows."

"Good point." She nods, conceding the point. "I'm ready whenever you are."

She's reverted back to that attitude of brisk efficiency that rubbed me the wrong way the day I met her, but it's even worse now. Now I know she's brisk and efficient, but she's also funny and warm and kisses like she means it.

Once we're on the road, I turn up the radio so the Christmas music can mask the awkward silence between us. I'm not sure how to break through it, and I'm considering whether she actually *wants* to talk about the kiss, but can't bring herself to initiate the conversation when she bursts into laughter.

"Did you see those inflatables?" she asks me, turning in her seat in an effort to see them again through the back window.

"I did."

"Be honest. The town *has* to get complaints."

"Oh, they do. Mostly from the homeowner. He's a bit of a cantankerous sort and after he's barked at the neighborhood kids for being too loud or cutting across his yard, he wakes up to find his inflatable reindeer in compromising positions."

I love the way her laughter fills the vehicle, drowning out the radio. "Why doesn't he get rid of the reindeer, then? He could find Christmas decorations that aren't so easy to make into inflatable orgies."

"I'm not sure anybody's asked him that, but it's a good question. He's stubborn, maybe? He likes having a reason to complain?"

Laughing together seems to have dispelled the awkward cloud hovering over us, and we talk about fair business as we cruise Main Street. It takes us a few passes because we can only drive so slowly without annoying other drivers and the amount of slush makes walking an unappealing option.

"I think the spot where the candy cane maze is going is the only trouble spot," I say once we've covered everything. "My dad and his buddies will take care of the sled runs. They do it every year, and we're already talked about it twice this morning."

"Oh look, there's a parking spot right in front of the General Store, and my cup is empty."

I have to brake a little suddenly to pull into the spot, but it's worth it when Whitney gives me a smile that'll keep me warm for the rest of the day. Of course, we can't just grab two coffees and run. Beth's in a mood to chat, and every time there's a lull and I think I can lure Whitney away, somebody comes in and strikes up a conversation with me.

By the time I get her back in the SUV, she's well-caffeinated, but already checking the time on her smartwatch. And when I make the right turn onto my street, she's scowling at her phone screen. It looks like an email app at a quick glance.

"Everything okay?" I ask as I pull into my driveway.

"I think so. I'm expecting some documents from the office and I haven't received them yet. Probably holiday-itis." She looks up, her phone screen going dark with a click. "Whose house is this?"

"Mine."

"Oh." She leans forward, trying to get a better look through the windshield. "You said it was near the fire station, but you're almost close enough to walk. It's cute."

Cute. It's probably her way of saying it's small, which it is. A small two-story Cape with a detached garage, both with light gray siding and white trim. It's simple, as is the landscaping, but I'm surrounded by trees and it has a nice porch.

"I got a good deal on it, and it checked all the boxes. Quiet road, but still close to town and work. Not in need of *too* much fixing up. And it got me out from under my parents' roof."

She looks at me thoughtfully, her head tilted. "I guess this is where I ask nosy, personal questions."

The way she wrinkles her nose makes me smile. "I thought I was in a serious relationship when I bought it. I probably should have guessed by her lack of interest in the process that *she* didn't think our relationship was that serious. And I guess I haven't gotten that far in a relationship since. How about you? Have you lived with anybody?"

"Nope. Where's the paint?"

I let her get away with the abrupt subject change because sitting in my vehicle, talking about past partners, is not how I want to spend my time with Whitney. "It's in the garage, but I'll unlock the house if you want, since you're on your second coffee."

She laughs. "Second coffee since I left the inn, so that would be great, actually."

I unlock the front door and let her know there's a half-bath and laundry room by the back door. I'm not worried about her wandering around the house. It's neat and a little on the spartan side, and I don't have anything stashed away that I wouldn't want her to find if she goes snooping.

And by keeping myself busy loading paint cans in the back of the SUV instead of giving her a tour, I can avoid being alone with her in a place where we can kiss without being interrupted.

A place that has a bed in it.

Nope. I hit the button for the liftgate and stand back as it slowly closes.

"Do you want me to lock this?" I hear Whitney call from the porch.

"Please."

She wasn't gone long enough to have snooped, which is a little disappointing, actually. It seems like if she was really into me, she would have poked around my house—maybe even taken a peek in my bedroom.

"Are you going to talk to the town hall about the snow?" she asks once we're back on the road.

"Yeah, I'll give them a call this afternoon."

"I hate to say it, but I still don't have those documents, so if you don't need me, I'll head back to the inn and find out what the problem is."

"The boss is away and it's almost Christmas," I say, and her sound of annoyance makes me chuckle. "We can swing by and get your car, but I'm going to the inn anyway to drop this paint off so we can paint tomorrow."

"Bring coffee."

"Of course. Did you pack any old jeans?"

She laughs. "I don't own any old jeans. I don't own any *new* jeans."

"Okay. That's…different. What do you wear when you're doing casual things? Like gardening or grocery shopping or hanging out with your family?"

"I rarely see my family, I live in an apartment so I don't have any dirt to dig in or grass to mow, and I do my grocery shopping on my way home from work without changing my clothes. I have business, business casual and relaxing at home clothes."

"Okay, what do you wear when you're relaxing at home?"

"Leggings and a T-shirt, usually."

Maybe that visual shouldn't jumpstart my heart rate, but it does. "Perfect. Did you bring any with you?"

"Yes, but—"

"There you go."

"I brought them to sleep in, so their current usage is as pajamas."

"You didn't bring pajamas to use as pajamas?"

"I don't wear pajamas to sleep in my own bed."

My brain shorts out, and I'm not sure how I keep the SUV on the road as images of Whitney, naked in bed, flash through my head. I strangle the steering wheel, trying to get myself under control.

I have to clear my throat twice before I can speak, though. "Yeah, that won't work for painting, I guess."

"Makes the clean-up easier, though," she says, and then she rests her hand on my arm as she laughs.

It's probably a good thing she goes straight from my SUV to her car when we get back to the station, and that I don't need her help moving the paint cans into the inn's garage because there's almost no chance I'd be able to keep my hands off of her in the state I'm in.

I'm going to stop by town hall, finish up my day, and then climb into a cold shower and stay there until it's time to see Whitney again.

CHAPTER
Nineteen

WHITNEY

Penny's eyes widen when I walk into the kitchen the next morning, following the scent of freshly brewed coffee.

"It's Casual Tuesday," I say, and she chuckles.

I'm wearing black leggings with a long sleeveless tunic over them. And I'm wearing a flannel shirt unbuttoned over that. After dealing with the office snafu yesterday afternoon, I went back to the General Store and bought myself warm socks and this red plaid flannel shirt, along with my coffee.

I guess it *is* convenient to find everything you need in one store.

"There will be painting involved," I add.

"Ah, Santa's sleigh. I've heard a lot about it because it's in the event barn with the inn's float, which means the library's float—which Erin always builds here—is in the garage. And it's Randy's spot in the garage that got bumped."

"Rob told me the sleigh got evicted from its usual storage by a project car. He has to park his SUV in his garage so it's always cleared off in an emergency. And it sounds like it can't live here."

Penny shrugged. "Somebody suggested putting up a storage shed behind the town barn, but nobody wants to pay for it."

I make a mental note to add it to the *Charming Lake* list Donovan asked me to keep. Problems stemming from a lack of funding in his adopted community have a way of quietly getting solved.

I've just finished my second cup of coffee—and a lovely cinnamon roll I nicked from Penny—when Rob's SUV pulls in. I shove my feet into my boots and meet him in the driveway, where he hands me one of the cups he brought from the General Store.

"Flannel looks good on you," he says, giving me a suggestive lift of one eyebrow that makes me blush.

"I try not to paint sleighs wearing anything dry clean only, as a rule."

After he unlocks the side door into the barn and reaches in to flip the light switch before stepping back to let me in, I have to admit the sleigh is impressive. Colorful and huge, like one of the fantastical sleighs from old children's book illustrations, it sits on a low trailer.

"Once it's in place, there's a skirt that goes around the bottom of the trailer, and wooden steps so the kids can get up there," he explains. "Most of the touch-ups are on this side, where everybody grabs to climb in, and their boots hit the side. Wear and tear type stuff."

"Let's do it," I say. "Right after I drink a little more of this coffee."

We've done the bigger patches and are barely an hour into the finer details—him working on the green holly leaves while I touch up the gold scrollwork—when his radio squawks and he has to go.

"Sorry. Hazard of the job. Will you be okay?"

"I'll keep working on it. I don't mind doing it alone."

"Those brushes are expensive. To clean them, you have to—"

I wave my hand toward the door. "I'll watch a YouTube video. Go."

When he finally returns, four hours later, I've finished cleaning the brushes to the best of my ability. And I think the sleigh touching-up is complete, which is good because he looks utterly exhausted, especially around the eyes.

He's also freshly showered, which probably means the call was an actual fire and not a medical call or an accident. Being careful not to touch the outside I'd touched up, he climbs up on the sleigh and sinks onto the bench seat next to me with a sigh of relief. I don't blame him. It's more like a leather sofa than a bench seat.

"Was it bad?" I ask quietly.

"Christmas tree fire. Old light strings." He gives me half a smile. "But it could have been worse. The family can stay with the grandparents and the living room was the only damage. The presents were already under the tree, though."

He pulls out a slip of paper and hands it to me. I scan the list of items, including a gaming system the parents had probably saved up for months to buy. After snapping a picture of the list and emailing it to myself so it'll be waiting when we're done painting, I tuck it in the pocket of my flannel shirt. I don't even need to run this purchase by my boss because I know his answer. "I can make these reappear."

"You would totally rock that elf costume," he teases, making me laugh.

"Come on now, my flannel and leggings don't do it for you?"

"Sweetheart, you could wear a potato sack and I would instantly develop a burlap kink."

Judging by the intense heat in his eyes when he says it, I'm not sure he's joking. Desire sizzles through my veins and

I know I should move—or at least look away—but I can't make myself.

I don't *want* to.

We've been sitting almost sideways, facing each other, and then one of us—I don't know if it's me or him, or maybe both—leans in and then we're kissing.

His mouth is hot and demanding, the kiss deep, and I'm so hungry for more, I throw my leg over his and straddle his lap without thought.

I moan when he pulls the elastic from my ponytail so he can bury his fingers in my hair. His other hand is clutching my ass as I move my hips, gliding along the erection that's prominent, even through his uniform pants.

Everything becomes a blur of desire and the need to have more of my skin in contact with his skin. The flannel shirt slides off easily, and then his mouth leaves mine to blaze a trail of kisses down my neck and over my bare shoulders.

Rob stops touching me just long enough for me to pull his shirt over his head, and then both his hands are cupping my breasts. My nipples are so taut and sensitive, his thumbs brushing them shoots pleasure through me, despite the fabric of the sleeveless tunic and my bra.

When he slides his hands under the tunic, trying to push it up and out of his way, I yank it off and toss it onto his discarded shirt. He doesn't even give me time to unfasten my bra—he pulls the cups down and draws my nipple into his mouth.

"Wait," I say breathlessly, threading my fingers through his hair to hold his head still. "We don't have any protection. I don't want to get into this and then have to stop."

His hand slides between my thighs. "We wouldn't necessarily have to stop *everything*."

I take Rob's chin in my hand, making him look me in the eye. "If I'm going to sully Santa's sleigh, I want it *all*. This is, like, naughty-list-forever level stuff, so it better be worth it."

Heat flares in his eyes. "I have a condom in my wallet."

I laugh and push him away. "You are *not* supposed to carry those things in your wallet, you know."

"I know." He gives me a sheepish grin. "But it's only been in there a couple of days. I guess you could say I'm an optimist."

"I can feel your optimism," I say, moving so my sex rubs the hard length of him. When he groans, I take mercy on him and stand so he can unfasten his pants and shove them down before sliding his wallet out of the back pocket. After digging the condom out, he tosses the wallet onto the shirts and opens the packet.

While he's taking care of business, I add my leggings and underwear to the pile. Then his hands are on my hips, hauling me back to astride his lap.

Rob's mouth closes over my nipple again, sucking hard, and I press down against him, trying to give my body what it's craving so desperately.

Then he rests his forehead against my sternum and trails his fingers lightly up the inside of my thigh. "Are you ready? Or do you need more?"

"Usually I'd make you work for it, but I just want you inside me now."

"Oh, thank the elves," he mutters, and that's why I'm giggling when he reaches between our bodies and guides himself into me.

My breath leaves me in a long, shuddering sigh as I lower myself slowly, rocking slightly until he fills me. Then I'm still, savoring the feeling, while his fingers grip my hips.

His breath is coming in bursts, and I know he's exerting all the self-control he can muster. I lean forward and kiss him, and his tongue plunges into my mouth. He fists his hand in my hair, not letting me go.

I start to move, lifting up and then slowly lowering

myself. The friction is delicious, but when his fingers tighten in my hair, I quicken the pace.

He groans, and then his hand is between us, his thumb stroking my clit. It sends me over the edge and as my muscles clench and I throw my head back, riding him through my orgasm, I'm not surprised he follows me right over the edge.

Panting, I collapse against him. Together, we wait to catch our breaths and for the tremors to fade while he kisses my neck and my shoulder and caresses my back.

"I wish I'd jerked off before I came back here," he said, sounding a little sheepish. "I would have liked to spend another hour or six inside of you."

I chuckle and then give him a quick kiss. "Sometimes fast and explosive is just what a body needs."

"My body definitely needed your body," he says as I straighten.

He holds the condom in place while I climb off of his lap, and as I pull my underwear on, he wraps it in a paint rag that was left on the floor of the sleigh. Then, after pulling up his boxers and pants, but not buttoning them, he pivots so he's lying across the bench with his legs over the side. I hope the paint's dry.

Then he pulls me on top of him, and as my body relaxes on his, I stop caring about the paint. He's a very comfortable man to lie on, and my body is so satisfied right now, my muscles are content to just melt into his warmth.

"We could just sleep here," he mutters into my hair.

"It's not even suppertime yet. Also, we're not nineteen and we've got about ten more minutes in this position before we need to call for help getting up. Nobody wants that."

"Good point. We could sneak upstairs to your bed. Nobody would even know I'm there."

"Again, it's not bedtime yet." I chuckle, pushing myself up. I need to get out of here before we get into it again and find ourselves a condom short. "Your vehicle's in the driveway, and it's pretty distinctive since it's bright red and has the CLFD logo on the doors and a light bar."

"My vehicle's often in the driveway."

"But the people inside know you're *not* inside with them."

"Penny won't say anything."

I'm sure he believes that, but he also doesn't have anything to lose if he's wrong. Though I have no idea how my boss would feel about me being naughty in Santa's sleigh with his brother-in-law, I'd rather not take the chance he'd question my professionalism.

"Time for you to go," I insist, taking his hand and pulling him to his feet. "Let's clean up. And make sure you get that rag from the sleigh because Charming Lake doesn't need a generational memory about the year a used condom was stuck to Santa's boot."

We laugh while quickly fixing our clothing situation, and then we make quick work of cleaning up the barn.

Then Rob's radio squawks again, and he listens to the information before cursing under his breath. "Dammit. I was going to drag you to the diner and use fries to lure you into letting me sneak into your room tonight, but this one's going to take a while."

"Raincheck," I say, even though I don't really mean it. Sneaking around in a barn is one thing, but I can't have Rob Byrne in my bedroom. "Go. I'll see you at the station in the morning."

He pulls me in for one quick—but fierce—kiss, and then he's gone.

CHAPTER

Twenty

ROB

I'm not alone in the equipment bay when Whitney arrives the next morning. Kevin, the youngest of the bunch, has been volunteering while working construction with his uncle, but he wants to start trade school and get his electrical license. I've written him some recommendation letters for some scholarships he's applied for, plus we've talked about his possible schedule because he wanted some reassurance we can make do without him sometimes (we can) and that he won't lose his spot (he won't).

After I introduce them, we make small talk for a few minutes—mostly Kevin asking Whitney about the big city—but he finally has to leave to pick up some things at the hardware store.

"I thought he'd never leave," Whitney says once the sound of his truck's engine fades away.

Her arms reach up to circle my neck and I pull her close for a very thorough first kiss of the day. Hopefully not the last, but just in case, I make it a good one.

"What's on the agenda today?" she says once I've reluctantly let her go. "You said to dress warmly, but you didn't say why."

"We're going to check out the sledding runs." I tuck a wisp of hair behind her ear. "Maybe we should go up to my office and figure out the rest."

She laughs and pushes at my shoulder. "No, we do *not* need to go upstairs to your office because I happen to remember you keep a bed in there, and we have too much to get done today."

"You'd rather go sledding than spend some time in that bed with me?"

"I'd rather spend time in that bed with you than do just about anything else," she says, and I'm not surprised my body heats, but I'd rather my heart stayed out of it. The pang in my chest isn't entirely welcome. "But we have to get through this list. Also, I thought you said your dad and his friends took care of the sled runs."

"They do. But I like to check their work because sometimes they think a jump or a corner might add to the kids' fun." I shrug. "Which it does, right up until a kid gets launched into the air and his parents collide trying to catch him."

"Did they get hurt?"

"No, but the mom wasn't impressed by the dad yelling at her that he waved her off, signaling it was his catch, and if she ever watched baseball, she would know that. They divorced a year later." I laugh at her expression. "Not because of the sledding. They really didn't like each other very much, even before that."

"So we'll definitely make sure they didn't add any jumps," she mutters.

"And since it's cold, it's a good idea to make a couple of runs to help compact them so they'll keep their shape when it warms up some."

"I'll enjoy watching you do that."

I let that slide, even though Whitney is absolutely going down the hill on a sled today. It'll be my reward for not being able to strip her clothes off.

Three hours later, her cheeks are rosy, and the sled runs are smooth. There are three runs built into the snow on the hill. There's a shallow, shorter one for the littlest kids. Then a medium one that would get the most use. And on the steepest part of the hill, a slightly longer one for the bigger kids and occasional adult.

My father and his crew had indeed tried to put some small jumps in the steepest of the three runs. After some debate between Whitney and I—her coming down on the side of that run being older kids who want to have fun and me coming down on the side of safety—we smoothed them down some, but left slight bumps.

"We should have bought a few extra candy canes to decorate the top of the hill," Whitney says, her hands on her hips as she looks it over.

"Well, here in Charming Lake, candy canes and sled hills aren't a good mix."

She snorts. "That sounds like a good story."

"One year, the organizers thought it would be fun to use red food coloring diluted with water in spray bottles to make red stripes down the runs, so they looked like candy canes. It was cold enough when they did it so the red stripes set up nicely. But then it was unseasonably warm the day of the fair itself."

"And the snow got mushy?"

"*Very* mushy. Josie Crane went down on her stomach and lost her sled halfway down, so according to my mother, she went to school every day looking like a murder victim."

She presses her gloved fingertips to her mouth. "Oh, no."

"In fact, a few years later, her coat turned up in the thrift shop and was bought to be part of a Halloween costume."

"The sled tracks must have looked gruesome."

I chuckle, shaking my head. "Very, from what I've been told. The town clerk gave a heads-up to the Department of Fish & Game and the state police in case somebody driving through town saw it, thought the worst, and called it in."

"And I thought small towns were boring."

"Nothing boring about the town's children leaving a holiday celebration looking like survivors of a slasher flick. All winter, most of the kids in town ran around with red stains on their coats and snow pants."

"And nobody bought the kids new coats?"

"Do you know how much good winter gear costs? When you have to save up and shop sales to get a decent coat, you're not throwing the budget out the window for a little red food coloring. And because it was basically the entire town going through it together, it was like an inside joke, I guess."

"And a fun story for future generations."

"That's the most important thing, of course." I grin at her. "Okay, time to test it."

"I'll watch while you do the test runs."

"So, if I come barreling down and I'm going to launch into the street, you'll catch me?"

She frowns, looking at the plow berms along the curb. "Is that a thing that can happen?"

"Not if my dad and his friends got the angles right. See how they all flattened out at the bottom? But…it's always a possibility, especially if it's a cold day." The horror on her face makes me laugh. "Because it faces a side street, we close that one for the fair, so nobody either hits or gets hit by a car. And there are always parents milling around the bottom, ready to catch runaway sleds."

"Fine." She sighs and yanks the red plastic saucer from my hand. "You don't even have a real sled. These things are a menace."

"They're also more fun."

She goes down the smallest run first, letting out a shriek at the top, but laughing at the bottom. Her excitement for the second one makes me laugh, but she hesitates at the top of the steepest run.

"What if it spins around so I'm backward?"

"That makes it even more fun. Haven't you gone sledding before?"

"Of course I have." She frowns down at me from the top of the hill, her hands in their familiar spot on her hips. "It's been a few years, you know. Do these saucers ever go up and over the edge of the runs? How many funny stories do you have about that?"

"Not a single one."

"Because it doesn't happen or because the stories don't have funny endings?"

I shouldn't laugh at her, but I can't help it. If she'd seen the places Jace and I used to sled—trees whizzing by in a blur —she'd probably hyperventilate. "As soon as you're at the bottom, we can go warm up."

That came out more suggestive than I intended. I'm not sure how she took it but, either way, it gets her butt on the saucer.

There's a heart stopping moment when her saucer rides high on the sloped wall of the run, just as she'd feared. But, despite the high-pitched squeak that comes out of her mouth, she stays calm and uses her body weight to correct the sled.

Right at the bottom, though, it spins and throws her into the snow, where she laughs so hard, she can't get up. Since I'm also doubled over with laughter, I can't really help.

When I do get myself under control and go to help her up, Whitney's already on her hands and knees. She pushes to her feet and I'm just about to take her arm when she steps forward, hits an icy spot, and ends up in my arms.

Both of us are laughing, and it takes all of my strength to keep us upright. And when she steadies herself and tips her face up—red from laughter and the cold and her eyes sparkling—I don't even think about it. I just press my lips to hers.

She kisses me back before snuggling against me. "You're very warm."

"Let's grab the saucer and get out of here."

Because she was such a good sport, I drive straight to the General Store. I run and grab two coffees while she sits in the warm vehicle.

"I used to go sledding with my mom," she tells me after taking a tentative sip of the hot liquid. "We had one of those old toboggans—you know, the wooden ones with the metal runners—and we'd fly on that thing."

I actually turn off on a side road to take a longer route back. Whitney rarely talks about herself, and I want to know *everything* about her.

"There was a great hill near us," she continues. "But we'd only walk all the way back up a couple of times. Then we'd pull the toboggan through the woods, collecting pinecones and whatever else struck our fancy."

"We have a couple of those toboggans at the inn. One of them is extra-long and my mom used to take pictures of all four of us sitting on it."

Once we're back at the station, she sets her coffee on a workbench and takes out her notebook while I put the saucer back in the Christmas Fair pile.

"Your family will be knocking out most of what's left on the list, I guess. The wrapping and stuff. We have all the forms and everybody knows where they're supposed to be." She gives me a sideways look. "Honestly, you could easily have done this without me."

"But it wouldn't have been nearly as much fun."

"That's a compliment I don't hear often."

I hold up my hands. "Then people aren't getting to know you."

She smiles, her cheeks flushing a pretty pink. "Penny's leaving after breakfast tomorrow and she said I might have a few hours of peace before the family starts arriving."

"When is Donovan due home?"

"Friday. He's cutting it close for the fair, but once that deal is off his desk, he'll have a much lighter workload in the weeks after the baby's born."

"So, a lighter workload for you?"

She laughs. "Except for the deluge from the *after-the-holidays* crowd when *after-the-holidays* actually arrives."

"Speaking of crowds." I lean against the truck and shove my hands in my pocket. "The inn's going to be full of my family until the fair is over and they'll expect me to take part in some of the goings-on."

"Oh." She catches her bottom lip with her teeth in a way that makes me want to kiss her. I'm getting used to that, though, because everything makes me want to kiss her. "I'd rather not…"

She lets her words fade away, but I know where she was going with them. It's disappointing, of course, but not surprising. Especially since one of my family members is her boss. "I get it."

When she hooks her finger over the neckline of my shirt, I let her pull me close. "Maybe they'll ding the sleigh while working on the other float and it'll need some quickie paint touch ups. Maybe we should go up to your office and discuss it."

I growl and claim her mouth with mine, trying to drown out the ticks of the clock counting down to this woman leaving me.

CHAPTER
Twenty~One

WHITNEY

There's probably a better use of my time than burrowing deeper under the covers and staring at the ceiling, but right now I can't imagine what that might be.

I should get up soon. I'm the only guest left in the inn, and I want to say goodbye to Penny and wish her a merry Christmas before she leaves. And I should check my email.

But mostly I want to stay where I am and think about what it would be like to have Rob snuggled up next to me.

My gut reaction is *I'd give anything for that*. But would I? Would I give up my entire life and my career to wake up next to Rob Byrne, here in Charming Lake?

There's no way he'd move to the city. I wouldn't even ask him to, because maybe he'd do it for me, but he'd be miserable. This is his *home* and his family is not only here, but the entire community.

And I've known the man for just shy of two weeks. Neither of us should be sacrificing anything for a person we just met. And sure, *when you know, you know* is probably an old adage because it can be true, but maybe it's more true for people who live in the same place.

This is ridiculous and I take it as a sign it's time for coffee. I get dressed and make my bed, and then I grab my notebook and go downstairs. Penny smiles at me when I walk into the kitchen.

"Good morning. There are muffins and some breakfast pastries, but I can make you breakfast before I leave, if you want."

"Oh, no. I'll have one of the pastries and lots of coffee. You must be excited to see your family."

"I am. My mom really goes all out for Christmas. And I hate missing the Charming Lake Christmas Fair, of course, but my town does a parade, too, and my family...well, tradition."

My mom goes all out for Christmas, too, I think with a shot of guilt. She never tries to make me feel bad about how hard I work or my focus on my career. And she's proud of me—I hear it in her voice and see it every time she looks at me.

But she misses me. And I miss her, and it's been too long since we've been together for Christmas.

Once Penny's gone and the big inn is empty, I open my notebook and pull up my email app. Donovan's wrapping up his business deal today, so I lose myself in monitoring the documents between their office and ours. There are also travel arrangements to check for the third time.

I'm pretty sure the deal is important to my boss, but getting home to his wife and son tomorrow—in time for the holiday celebration—is more important.

Hitting the bottom of the coffee pot drags me out of the work, and I decide I'll occupy my time until the Byrne family descends on us by organizing the wrapping paper and other things needed for the Santa Fund gifts.

I've just finished washing my coffee cup and the spoon

when the door into the kitchen opens and a small child runs in, trips on the thick mat, and falls on his face.

Luckily, Sam's wearing enough puffy winter wear to cushion his fall because he's already pushing himself to his knees when his mother comes in behind him. No sign he's about to burst into tears or start screeching.

"I told you not to run," Nat says, sounding exhausted. After closing the door behind her, she bends and grabs the back of Sam's coat to haul him upright. "Hi, Whitney."

"Good morning."

"He's so excited about seeing everybody here and I told him over and over it wasn't time yet, but he wouldn't stop. So here we are, for no reason, because—believe it or not—being a thousand months pregnant can wear on the nerves and I couldn't take the *mommy mommy mommy* anymore."

I have to step up here. I know it, and not just because she's my boss's wife, but because she's a woman who's obviously worn thin and needs a little help. But I'm not great with kids and I've never been alone with an extremely pregnant woman before.

After glancing at my smartwatch to see the time, which flew by while I was buried in my usual routine, I realize nerves might not be the only reason for the queasiness I feel. I'm running on a lot of coffee and very little food.

"I was just going to take some cookies and coffee into the front room to relax for a while," I lie. "Do you want something to drink?"

"Cookies," Sam squeals, and I wince. I probably should have spelled that word out, like I've seen other adults do.

"I'd love a hot cocoa, but you don't have to make it for me."

"I've got it." I wave her off. "That sounds good, actually. I'll make two."

"Can you put a little of mine into a cup with a lot of milk for Sam?"

"Of course."

There's a pretty tray on the counter that Penny would probably use, but I'm not sure about my ability to balance two hot drinks, a lukewarm drink, and a plate of cookies on it. Instead, when the beverages are done, I carry theirs out and then go back for mine and the cookies.

I've barely sat down when Sam comes and leans against my knee, holding up a cookie.

"What does he want?" I ask his mother, because I'm not sure if kids just eat their food while leaning on people they barely know.

"Well, he's handing you the cookie, so he wants you to take it, and if you don't, he'll cry. And you might think it's safe to assume he wants you to eat it because he gave it to you, but if you do, he'll cry because you ate his cookie."

"So it's a trap."

"Yes."

I take the cookie from the tiny manipulator, not sure what to do with it as he giggles and runs off. It's a little awkward, sitting with a cookie I'd very much like to take a bite of, while he goes back and grabs another cookie.

He brings that one to his mother and then returns to me. Leaning on my knee again, grinning up at me, he takes his cookie back.

"You look so much like your uncle Rob with that cheeky grin," I say, unable to keep from smiling in return.

When he runs off, trailing cookie crumbs, to pull a basket of trucks out of a cabinet I hadn't even noticed, I turn my attention back to Natalie.

I really don't like the way she's looking at me—like she's pretty sure I have a secret and she wants to know what it is.

"So you and Rob, huh?"

I should probably deny it. I mean, lots of people tell kids they look like somebody else in the family. And I was the one who asked him to keep our relationship from his family.

She arches her eyebrow, waiting, and I feel the blush across my face and chest. "The Christmas fair is going to be a success. We work well together."

"Indeed." She smiles, a sly tilt to her lips. "You were probably still eating your lunch when I got a text telling me the city girl was in the diner, eating out of Rob's hand."

"Okay, that's not—" I pause, because that actually did happen. "He wanted me to try salt and vinegar on fries, so it was just a taste test of his before I ate my own."

"I would have taken the test fry out of his hand, but that's just me."

I do *not* want this conversation getting away from me. "But then I would have had vinegar on my fingers and what if I didn't like it?"

She shrugs, giving me an amused look that almost matches her brother's. "Ah. I didn't realize they forgot to bring you napkins."

My mind spins, trying to think of some way to change the subject with a topic more interesting to her than her brother hand-feeding fries to the city girl. I've got nothing.

Suddenly Natalie sucks in a breath, and when she exhales, there's a faint keening sound in that breath. Then she leans forward, hands on her stomach, as her face contorts in pain and panic floods every cell in my body.

I have no idea what to do.

CHAPTER

Twenty-Two

ROB

This is the second time since becoming fire chief that I've turned into the driveway of the Charming Inn with the red lights flashing and two of my wheels barely in contact with the asphalt.

The first time, a call came in that a woman my mother's age had taken a tumble on the stairs. It turned out to be a guest—and her only injury was to her dignity—but it took a solid two hours for my pulse to return fully to normal.

I think something is wrong with Nat. She's in pain, I think. Can you come?

By the time I burst into the house and find Nat sitting peacefully on the sofa, I'm afraid I'll need medical attention myself. I stand in the sitting room doorway, bag in hand, and try to assess the situation while I catch my breath.

Nat looks absolutely fine. Uncomfortably pregnant, but she's smiling and I don't see any signs of distress.

Sam is on the floor with his trucks, and there's nothing wrong with him.

And then I look at Whitney. Her face is pale, and it honestly looks as if she just fought an entire war, single-handedly and unarmed. She's on her feet, but weaving slightly, and I take a step toward her.

"Are you going to pass out? Your skin's got a gray tint thing happening and I don't think you've blinked since I got here."

She blinks. Once.

Nat tries to laugh, even though she mostly holds her stomach and makes a pained sound of amusement. "Whitney pulled up a YouTube video on how to deliver a baby at home in case you didn't make it in time."

"In time for what?" I scowl at my sister. "You're not actually in labor, are you? If you are, we're calling an ambulance because I'm not going there."

"I'm not in labor."

"Aren't you an EMT?" Whitney asks, some of her color returning. "Somebody said you're a firefighter *and* an EMT."

"I'm an AEMT, so *can* I deliver a baby? Yes, in an emergency. Am I going to deliver Nat's baby? Absolutely not."

My sister barks out a laugh. "He's afraid of my vagina."

"Oh, he's not afraid of—" Whitney starts, and then her words choke off. She's definitely got color back in her cheeks now. "You mean *your* vagina, in particular. Of course. Because you're his sister—not just…in general."

I'd tell her to stop talking, but the damage is already done. The look Nat gives me is loaded with amusement and speculation, and my life just got two hundred percent more complicated. My sister is currently adding two plus two and coming up with four and, sure, that's the right answer, but I'd rather that math never came up in the first place. I'll never hear the end of it now.

"I'm going to check your vitals," I tell Nat in an effort to change the subject to anything but vaginas.

"I swear it's just random Braxton Hicks contractions," she says, trying to fend me off. "I'm absolutely fine, Rob."

"I'm taking your blood pressure. The more you fight me on it, the higher it'll be."

She surrenders with a sigh and an unnecessarily dramatic eye roll. I check her over, paying more attention to her than to the numbers. She's relaxed, her breathing is calm, and her blood pressure's just fine. Her ankles look good. Even with her being one of the most important women in my life, nothing flags as remotely alarming.

I pack my equipment away in the bag. "Everything looks good, but you call me or Mom or literally anybody if that changes, okay?"

"Okay, but it's just Braxton Hicks," Nat tells me again. "And now that we've established that, you can relax and hang out with us."

There's no way I'm letting a very bored, very pregnant woman get a foothold in a matchmaking scheme. "I should get back. I was actually in the middle of something when the call came in."

"Wait. You can't go," Whitney says, and there's a very uncharacteristic pleading note to her voice. "You have to stay."

"Nat's not in labor and, like I said before, I was in the middle of something." It wasn't anything important, but it was better than being here.

"You can't leave me here alone with a small child and an extremely pregnant woman who's making strange noises while rubbing her stomach." She reaches out and clutches the front of my shirt. "Maybe one of those I could handle, but I can't do both. Or you can stay here and I'll go finish whatever *you* were doing."

"And if a call comes in, are you going to put out the fire?"

"Yes, I will. I feel a lot more qualified to be in charge of a fire scene than handling what was happening in that video."

She's so earnest, it's hard not to laugh at her, but I do my best. Judging by the increased pressure on my shirt, though, I'm doing a bad job of hiding my amusement. Behind Whitney, Nat has her face pressed into a throw pillow, but her shoulders are shaking.

"Rob," Whitney whispers, her head tilted back so she can pin me with her pleading gaze. "I know you deal with this kind of pressure every day, but I don't and the stakes are so—"

"I'll stay." Since Nat's already figured out that math problem, I confirm it by tugging my shirt out of Whitney's fist and then wrapping my arms around Whitney. She's trembling and I hold her close. "Everybody's okay, and I can hang out for a little while."

After a moment, the shaking subsides, but she only buries her face harder against me. "I'm so embarrassed."

"There's nothing to be embarrassed about," I murmur into her hair.

"I overreacted. Like, *wildly* overreacted. I shouldn't have texted you like that."

While the text message had probably taken a year or two off my life, she shouldn't regret asking for help if she needed it. "Listen, when we're called to an emergency that turns out to be a false alarm, that's a good day. What makes for the worst days is when people *don't* call us because they think they can handle it or that it's not that bad and they don't want to look foolish, and by the time they call us, it's too late. Even if we weren't talking about my sister and the niece I haven't even met yet, you did the right thing."

I feel her stiffen slightly, as if she just realized we're putting on a show for my sister—her boss's wife—so I'm not surprised when she pulls away.

"Okay." She takes a deep breath and lets it out slowly. "Do you want something to drink? Or some cookies. And unlike your adorable nephew, I'll actually let you eat them."

We all laugh, breaking the tension in the room, and Whitney goes into the kitchen to pour me a coffee. I'm not surprised she's barely out of sight before Nat is giving me her best nosy sister expression.

I shake my head. Not only do I not want to have a conversation about Whitney when she's right there in the kitchen, but I have no idea what I'd even say.

Yes, I think Whitney might be *the one*. Actually, I'm almost sure of it.

No, I'm not going to say that out loud to anybody because Whitney has a life and a career she loves in New York City. I can't ask her to give that up.

Natalie holds her hands out, palms up, in a silent demand for more of a reaction. I shake my head again and she scowls.

I'm saved from the probability she's going to start using words when Erin walks in, bringing a blast of cold air with her. Considering the library isn't supposed to be closed right now, I'm surprised to see her.

After slipping out of her boots and dumping her coat on top of the pile, she flops onto the couch next to Nat. "You don't look like you're in labor. One of our patrons said he saw Rob flying in here with his lights and sirens going."

"Oh no," Whitney wails from the kitchen, confirming my fear she'd be able to hear any conversation happening in the front room. "The whole town knows?"

"It was Braxton-Hicks, but Whitney wanted to be sure," Natalie explains. Then she raises her voice. "And we appreciate her erring on the side of caution."

"Always better to be safe than sorry when it comes to babies," Erin agrees in a similarly loud voice.

When Whitney comes out with a coffee and a couple of cookies for me, my sisters have already pivoted to a discussion about the library's float. Whitney sits in an armchair and when she meets my eye, I give her a smile.

To my relief, she smiles back. Her body language is

relaxed, and it looks like she's starting to see the humor in the situation, which is good. Putting up with the Byrne family requires a healthy sense of humor, plus I don't want her feeling uncomfortable.

I'm only halfway through my coffee when my radio squawks and I have to leave in a hurry. But not so much of a hurry that I don't pause at the door, listening to the sound of Whitney's voice and laughter blending with my sisters'.

CHAPTER

Twenty-Three

WHITNEY

By the time Rob texts me the following day about the candy cane maze, I'm desperate to get out.

The inn definitely isn't empty anymore. Justine Donovan —my boss's mother—and her wife, Judy, arrived about two hours after Natalie and Sam showed up. Then Rob's parents, Stella and Randy, arrived with Nana Jo. It was a lot of introductions, but they were all super nice and, of course, had heard a lot about me. There was definitely a *practically one of the family* vibe that made me vaguely uncomfortable due to the amount of time I spend thinking about Rob.

His sister Layla and her two daughters, Mel and Elsa, were staying in one of the rooms, as well. When Erin arrives after work tonight, she's going to stay in Penny's room. I offered to switch rooms, since I'm an employee and so she could be nearer to her family, but she muttered something about the distance being a feature and not a bug, waving me off.

Breakfast this morning was loud and chaotic, especially

with two girls who still had to go to school, and the energy switched from elegant inn to family Christmas gathering overnight.

It's a little exhausting, and Rob's text was a perfect reprieve.

There's some kind of popcorn being made and Mr. Wilson is on his plane, so I have some time. I'm not sure how the parking situation is right now. It might be a car version of Jenga out there.

I'll pick you up in 20 minutes. First stop is the General Store.

Yesssss. I love yo…

I stop typing and stare at the words I've written on my screen. Then I delete them so quickly, I'm shocked I didn't sprain my thumb.

Yessss. Then the coffee emoji.

That's better, though I'm not sure why I'm so thrown by the message I almost sent. It's the casual sort of thing one might say when offered coffee. *Yes, I love you.*

But things don't always land the same way in written form. And that's all it was. It can't be that it was wrong to type those words because they felt too real to me.

I haven't known him long enough, have I?

I'm ready to go when I get the next text from him. *I'm outside. Can we make our escape without me coming in and getting sucked into the Byrne family chaos?*

Without even bothering to reply, I slip out the kitchen door and climb into the passenger seat of his SUV. I barely have my seatbelt fastened before he's pulling out of the driveway.

I would have liked a kiss, but I make do with his hand reaching over to cover mine.

"Is it bad in there?" he asks, humor in his voice. "I feel bad for not going in, but once you're in there, it's hard to get out."

"Everybody's so nice, but it's a lot."

"I bet Beth can whip us up something that will help," he

says, and then he gives me a grin that threatens to stop my heart.

Two hours later, we've stuck a bunch of two-foot-tall candy canes in the snow covering a patch of grass on the front lawn of the library. We used the pattern we sketched out several days ago, but I'm not sure we did it right.

"It's not much of a maze." I put my hands on my hips, looking over the very short candy canes we've anchored in the snow. "You're not supposed to be able to see the entire thing before you start."

"It's for the little ones," he says, his voice thick with amusement. "We're not really looking to give them candy cane trauma. And the parents like being able to see them."

"That's a good point. I guess letting Sam loose in an actual maze of candy canes wouldn't go over well with the Wilsons."

"Also, we have teen volunteers who spend most of their time sticking the candy canes back in the snow after the kids knock them down. If we actually put a lot of time and labor into making the maze, it would make you cry."

"I'll check it off, then."

"I don't think there's anything left we can do out here until we start herding the feral cats that are the parade participants."

"When you say 'out here', you mean what?"

He sighs and gives me an exaggerated look of defeat, slumped shoulders and all. "It's time to go back to the inn."

As soon as we return, Rob is gathered up by his family, and Natalie pulls me aside.

"Donovan's delayed in New York, but he said he should be on his way home in no time and that we shouldn't worry."

The blood drains from my face. "I'm so sorry. I should have been on top of that."

"I know you're very good at your job, but I don't think

maintaining every plane he might travel on is part of the job description."

"It's my job to know if he's been delayed and find a way to smooth that out for him, not to hear it from his wife." I was playing with plastic candy canes while Donovan Wilson was experiencing a travel glitch, and that's unacceptable.

Natalie laughs and grabs my arm. "You look like you're going to pass out, Whitney. Come on. Donovan called me to check on me, as husbands do. He mentioned the delay, and I told him you were working on the fair setup with Rob. Then we talked about Sam and the baby and all the chaos of the family. It's a short delay and if he needed you, he would text you. Have a cookie or something. Relax."

Hours later, my body aches from sitting on the floor, wrapping gifts with the rest of the family, but I'm thoroughly relaxed. It's hard not to be when you're surrounded by joyful, laughing people. The family has a system to keep track of the gifts being wrapped, so I'm able to fold and tape without worrying about it.

And every single time Rob catches my eye, he gives me a look that actually makes me wish some kind of fair-related emergency would come up so we could run off together. Maybe somebody knocking over all the candy canes. Or somebody trying to reenact the year of the slasher film with red food coloring.

It's not until a door slams that I realize I've lost track of time. Sam runs in, tugging his dad's hand while Donovan's hand is holding Natalie's.

"Look who we found on the porch," Natalie says, beaming.

I'm horrified to realize I totally forgot about my boss and his travel woes, and here I am, sitting on the floor. I have ribbons around my neck—a necklace made by Mel—and Elsa and Sam had fun sticking bows to my hair.

I look and feel like anything *but* an excellent assistant.

My phone buzzes and I pull it out to find a text from Rob, who's only about four feet from me.

He'll keep them distracted. Let's go touch up the paint on the sleigh.

I lock my phone instantly, hoping nobody else in the room could see my screen. Part of me wants desperately to sneak out the back with Rob for a little private time in the sleigh.

But the other part of me is too busy beating myself up for dropping a work ball to feel anything. I need to focus on my job, and making sure my boss and his family, and I shake my head at him.

He looks at me for a long moment before his gaze flicks to Donovan. Then he gives me what I hope is an understanding smile and goes back to wrapping.

CHAPTER
Twenty~Four

ROB

I wake up after a restless night to a gorgeous winter day. Charming Lake couldn't have asked for better weather for an outdoor celebration.

I spent the night at the station, staying up late to make sure the engine was polished and gleaming. All the wreaths had to go on it, and the sparkly garland run through the ladders.

When I finally stretched out on the slightly lumpy twin bed, all I could think about was Whitney. I'd seen her face when Donovan walked in—the realization she'd been so caught up in the Christmas spirit she'd forgotten about her job for a few minutes.

She'd been withdrawn after that, despite my efforts to get her to sneak out. And when we'd started decorating the family Christmas tree, she'd excused herself and gone to her room. With all my family around, I couldn't come up with a good reason to go upstairs to check on her.

I'd tried to convince myself to sleep by telling myself it

was for the best because she was leaving soon, anyway. That had grossly backfired because all I could think about was how empty my days were going to feel without Whitney in them.

So my mood today isn't as pleasant as the weather, but I'm determined—if this is the end between Whitney and me—I'm going to make sure she enjoys the hell out of the Christmas fair.

Since it's not easy to navigate the main street once everybody starts piling in, I drive the engine to the elementary school parking lot, where the parade is being staged. I park it in the general vicinity of its assigned spot, and head on foot toward the General Store.

Of course Whitney beat me to it.

She's just turning away from the counter when I walk in, and she has a coffee cup in each hand. When she sees me, she stops, her lips curving into a warm smile.

I burst out laughing.

She's wearing the sweater. And she even hit the button so all the lights attached to it are glowing. She laughs with me, and then shimmies so the bells jingle.

Then I have to step out of the way of another customer, and Whitney joins me so we're standing off by ourselves. There's no trace of last night's reserve, and I want to kiss her so badly, I have to curl both hands around the coffee she hands me to keep from touching her.

"I told you I'd wear it." She laughs and the bells jingle again. "I actually kind of like it."

Then I look down and realize she's wearing jeans. And actual winter boots. "Jeans? How casual of you."

"Your sisters were very insistent I be dressed properly for today. The jeans are Lyla's and the boots are Erin's. And I'm wearing merino wool long underwear, also Erin's. I tried to tell them it's not all that cold today, but they said I'd be spending hours outside, not just going from house to car."

She takes a sip of her coffee with an appreciative hum that she also makes during sex.

Not that I'm thinking about that. And certainly not today.

"It *is* warm in here, though." She looks around. "They're already busy."

"It's always a good day for businesses along the main street." I lead the way toward the door, holding it open for her.

"I already did a quick walk around," she tells me. "Everything seems to be in place. Even the candy canes."

"The teens in Charming Lake can get up to no good, like teens anywhere, but I don't remember anybody ever messing with the Christmas fair."

"Makes our job easier. So what's next?"

I snort, hating to pop her festive bubble. "The not so easy part. I hate to say it, but the hour before the parade starts is… intense. You might regret not telling Donovan to shove this particular assignment where the Christmas lights don't shine."

She laughs, clearly not believing me. "We set the order and everybody got a copy. It'll be fine."

It is *not* fine.

Once we start trying to organize the floats, trucks, tractors, one school chorus, various sports teams, farm animals, and more, I don't see Whitney again until three minutes before the police chief is supposed to lead us out of the parking lot. I wouldn't say she's hiding, exactly, but it was difficult to find her pressed against the side of the engine, away from the crowd.

"Are you shirking your duties?" I tease, making her jump.

"Rob, you wouldn't even—" She throws up her hands. "A goat kept trying to eat my sweater. Two men got in an argument because apparently one guy's diesel exhaust or something stinks and wouldn't switch places. And either one family has a set of septuplets or I sent the same girl back to the chorus float at least seven times. One more time, and I was going to duct tape her to it."

"Long, dark hair, with penguins on her scarf?" She nods. "I sent her back three times myself."

"Jerry is a *fantastic* Santa, though," she says. "I had my doubts about the padding, but he looks incredible."

"He loves doing it, too. And if you want to see it all, you can join the family on the sidelines. I can tell you where they are."

She tilts her head. "I'm not riding in the fire truck with you?"

I definitely want her next to me. No question. "You don't get to see much of the parade when you're in it. The school chorus sings from the back of the inn's float, and there's a lot of other fun stuff to see."

Her eyes crinkle when she smiles. "I'd rather ride with you."

"Okay, then." Having her look at me like that hurts with an intensity I'm not sure I'll survive. I need to keep things light and pretend I'm okay. "It's probably a good thing you didn't wear that elf costume. You climbing up into the engine would have been a show Charming Lake talked about for generations."

Even though she looks more frazzled than I thought was possible, she laughs. "Is there a prize for the best display?"

I move closer to her. "Not officially, but as the organizer, I'm sure I could come up with something."

The chirp of a cruiser siren makes my shoulders drop. "Time to roll."

She follows me around to the other side of the engine. "I don't think we're ready."

I open the door and gesture for her to climb up. "We've done what we can. Believe it or not, once we start moving, everybody kind of falls into line."

She looks skeptical, but she climbs into the cab. "This is really high up."

When I climb into my seat, she's looking around in fascination, taking it all in. "Do me a favor and don't press any buttons."

"But think of all the fun stories about the year the city girl was in the fire truck."

I laugh, shaking my head. Once the parade starts rolling, though, I have to pay more attention to what I'm doing, and less to my very-sexy-in-that-sweater passenger. It's actually a little nerve-wracking driving a thirty-thousand-plus pound vehicle at a slow speed through what looks like the entire community. There's a reason the tow truck—decked out in LED lights with Christmas rock blaring from its speakers—is assigned to the spot in front of me. At least I can see it.

We have the windows down, both of us waving. And periodically, I do a couple of short bursts with the horn to signal to the parents of little ones I'm about to let the siren wail.

When we near the booth I was looking for, I get Whitney's attention and point. "See that booth? No matter what, do *not* miss out on Mrs. Johnson's snickerdoodles. I probably should have written that in your notebook for you days ago."

She side-eyes me. "Nobody writes in my notebook but me. Anyway, Mrs. Johnson, like your lieutenant?"

"Yeah, she's Tim's mother. There have been fights over her snickerdoodles, no matter how many she bakes in advance." He chuckles. "Okay, not exactly with fists flying, but there's been some pushing and shoving and very unfortunate name calling over the years."

"Got it. My first stop is snickerdoodles."

I think about how I felt when I saw her this morning, turning to face me wearing that ridiculous sweater, holding two coffee cups and her face lit up, and my heart aches.

Once she's gone, how long will it be before that feeling of

being a couple fades? When Beth hands me a coffee, how much and how long will it hurt that there's only one?

Then there's a sudden stop because somebody's dog slipped their collar and has decided its job is to herd the FFA's prize-winning cow away from the parade.

As I wait for them to get the scene under control, I look over and find Whitney staring at me. Her expression is serious—thoughtful, even—and I'm not sure what that means.

But when our eyes meet, she smiles, looking gorgeous and festive and happy, and I don't ask her what she was thinking about.

CHAPTER
Twenty-Five

WHITNEY

Riding in a fire truck in a small town Christmas parade was something I'd never imagined happening to me, but as Rob helps me down out of the engine, I'm so overcome by the holiday spirit, I want to throw my arms around him and kiss him like we're under the mistletoe.

I don't, of course. There are a ton of people watching. But I want to.

"The next part is boring," he tells me once my boots hit the ground. "Just making sure everybody leaves their stuff in a way that doesn't block other people before they walk over to the fair, and then I usually park the engine behind the cruiser blocking off the street because it looks festive. You should go get us some snickerdoodles and then find my family. I'll meet up with them as soon as I can."

It feels strange to walk away from him without a goodbye kiss, or at least a touch, and as I make my way through the crowd in search of the renowned snickerdoodles, I remind myself I have to get used to it. I'm not going to have him in my life for very much longer.

Even surrounded by the community's revelry, I suddenly feel sad and a little empty. I'm not sure I've ever dated—or whatever I'm calling it—a man like Rob before. He makes me laugh and when I'm with him, I relax, but he doesn't do it at the expense of what's important to me, like my job.

I wonder if we'd met under difference circumstances, if we'd have taken the time to get to know each other. Not that it matters, because if I'd run into him in the city, I might not even have noticed him. I'm in a strange place here in Charming Lake. I'm working, and yet it's not at all like my usual job.

Either way, it's depressing, so when I get to the front of the snickerdoodle line, I buy four of the snickerdoodles, which she puts in a tiny paper bag for me because I want to wait and enjoy them with Rob. For some reason, I think he'll be disappointed if he doesn't get to see my reaction to the first bite.

When I join the Byrne family, Mel and Elsa are in the middle of begging to go sledding. Sam, of course, wants to go just because his cousins want to. And when they're all told to wait for Uncle Rob because he *loves* to take them sledding, I bite my lip to keep from laughing.

When Donovan turns and sees me, he smiles. "That's a very festive sweater. Not your usual style, but I like it."

"It makes Rob happy," I say, and when my boss's eyebrows shoot for his hairline, I realize I've made a huge mistake. "He tricked me into wearing it, believe it or not."

"Oh, I'm married to his sister. Trust me, I believe it," he replies in a voice so warm with affection, it makes my heart ache.

"What have you got there?" he asks, nodding toward the paper bag I'm holding.

I clutch it to my chest. "Nothing."

"Are those Mrs. Johnson's snickerdoodles?" His eyes narrow. "How much do you want for them?"

"They're not for sale."

He laughs. "Come on, Whitney. Everything's for sale."

"They're for Rob." Usually I'd be confident my boss isn't the kind of jerk who'd use his power over my income to steal cookies from me, but Rob did warn me people can get rowdy when it comes to the snickerdoodles.

The corners of his lips twitch and he leans close so he can lower his voice. "I have three in a bag in my pocket, for me and Natalie and Sam."

I also lower my voice. "You miscalculated, then, because Natalie is going to take that bag into the bathroom, lock the door, and eat all three."

His laughter draws the attention of everybody else, including Rob, who's just appeared at my side. "What's funny?"

"I was trying to buy Whitney's snickerdoodles," Donovan says before I can answer. "But she said they're for you, so I guess I can't afford them."

A look passes between the two men that I can't quite decipher, and I know I'm missing some subtext in what Donovan said. But I'm distracted from worrying about how much Natalie has told my boss by Sam jumping up and down.

"I want to go on the sleds!"

"You were volunteered, by the way," I tell Rob, grateful for the subject change.

"Actually, I think I'll take the kids over," Donovan says. "You two did all the work for the fair. You should get to enjoy it."

Another pointed look passes between the men, and then Donovan gathers up Sam and tells the rest of the family they're heading for the sled runs.

Rob tucks his hand under my arm and subtly steers me away from the family before we can get sucked into the excitement. Because of the crowd, I'm a little turned around and I don't realize where we're heading until I see the General Store in front of us. Once we've gotten our coffees, Rob guides us to some hay bales that have been placed around town for people to sit on.

"Another new experience," I tell him as I make myself comfortable. "I'll have to thank your sister for the jeans because I don't think this straw would work with leggings."

"A bit prickly, I'd imagine." He takes the paper bag and peeks inside before giving me that heart-stopping grin. "*Four*? Did you have to fight anybody?"

"I'm not going to answer that."

He laughs and pulls out a snickerdoodle, handing it to me. "Did you try one yet?"

"No, I wanted to wait for you."

I'm rewarded for my restraint with a warm smile so potent my body reacts as though he's caressed my cheek. "Trust me, they're worth waiting for."

Because I know he won't eat his own cookies until he's seen me taste mine, I take a big bite of the snickerdoodle. When I close my eyes with a deep moan of appreciation, I'm not exaggerating.

"I told you!" He took his cookie out of the bag and devoured it in two bites.

"If I'd known they were this good, I would have hid behind a building and eaten all four."

He laughs, taking the other two cookies out of the bag and handing me one. "I believe you would have."

We take our time savoring these cookies and drinking our coffees. There are plenty of people to watch, and with his leg pressing along the length of mine, I'm not in a hurry to move.

"I should probably warn you," he says, "we have a tradition for *after* the Christmas fair, too."

"Of course you do."

"We hang out at the inn and watch *Elf* while we eat baked macaroni and cheese."

"Maybe I'll sneak a bowl of it up to my room when nobody's looking."

"Nope, that's cheating. You only get the carbs and cheese if you sit through the movie."

"Rob, my job here is done. And that's your family time. I really don't belong there."

His shoulders straighten, and he frowns. "What? Of course you belong there."

Oh, how I wish he meant that the way my heart took it. "I'm not family. I work for your brother-in-law."

"You did most of the work. And you helped with the wrapping and...no. I want you there."

There was something about the way he said it that twisted me up inside—like maybe he *did* mean it the way I wished he would. "Okay. I'm in."

He gives me a sheepish grin. "Okay. But in that case, I have an additional warning, actually."

"Maybe we should get some *hazard ahead* stickers printed up for your family."

"We'd definitely put some on the casserole dishes. The Byrne Family Baked Macaroni and Cheese recipe is...not great." He wrinkles his nose in a most adorable way. "Actually, the recipe's probably fine, but the execution would get us booted off a reality cooking show before the first commercial break."

After we're finished with the cookies and coffee, we wander around the Charming Lake Christmas Fair for hours, and it's great to see the community enjoy the work Rob and I did. We watch the preschoolers having a blast in the candy cane maze. The sledding runs are a huge success. And I actually tear up a little watching the kids climb on to the sleigh to have their photos taken with Santa and get their Santa Fund gifts.

By the time the festivities start winding down, my feet hurt and my stomach aches from laughing. I don't mind, though, because between the joyful vibe of the town and the man I shared it with, the Charming Lake Christmas Fair was the best day of my life.

But it doesn't take long, once everybody's back at the inn, for that festive glow to fade. And it starts with the thought that's running through my head as the Byrne family pulls out the massive casserole dish of baked macaroni and cheese, triggering fake smiles all around.

I wish my mom was here. She would love this family and their holiday shenanigans.

The truth is, *I* love this family and their holiday shenanigans. But I don't think I can go into the family room with them and watch a Christmas movie and whatever else their traditions call for.

I can't be a part of their family gathering because I'm not family. But I also can't join in and pretend I'm just Donovan's assistant being included out of kindness because Rob feels like more than that to me and I'm not sure we can hide that.

As much as it hurts, the time has come for me to start disentangling myself from Rob and his family.

When he tries to hand me a bowl, I shake my head. "I'm still stuffed from all the fair food I ate today. I think I'm going to head up to my room."

"You'll miss the movie."

I force a smile. "I know how it ends."

When his gaze holds mine, searching, I know he wants to question my decision, but there's only so much he can say when surrounded by his family. "You feeling okay?"

"Yeah. Just tired and very much not hungry. And I need to start making plans to head back to the city."

The words land the way I knew they would—I can see it in the way his jaw clenches and his shoulders drop. "Sure. If you change your mind, the mac will be in the fridge and we'll be in the family room."

I nod before he or anybody else can say anything more, and I'm a little afraid I might burst into tears. I keep it together all the way to my room, though, where I immediately strip down to my underwear.

I don't put on music and dance it out, though.

Instead, I stretch out on the bed and stare at the ceiling as though I'll find something there to ease the utter panic running through my mind.

I don't want to leave Charming Lake.

And I *really* don't want to leave Rob.

But then I think of all of my striving for more in high school. The striving in college. I remember how hard it was to climb every single rung of the corporate ladder.

Then I roll onto my stomach so the pillow can absorb my tears.

CHAPTER

Twenty-Six

ROB

I'm not in a great mood when Whitney shows up at the fire station the next morning.

I didn't sleep worth a damn. The movie was ruined. The baked macaroni and cheese was ruined. Right now it felt as if all of Christmas was ruined.

She'd as good as said goodbye last night, and I wasn't even sure she would show up today. I knew it was coming—I'd reminded myself so many times Whitney's stay in Charming Lake was temporary—but that didn't make it hurt any less.

What will make it all hurt a lot *more* will be spending the day with Whitney and falling back into our easy way with each other, only to be reminded again that she's leaving.

I can't do it.

"Didn't expect to see you today," I say in lieu of a proper greeting, and my voice is admittedly a little more harsh than it needed to be.

She frowns and sets my coffee down on the bench when I

don't go and take it from her. "Why? There's a lot of wrapping up to do, I'm sure."

"Your job was to help me put on the Christmas fair. You don't have to help break it down. The guys and I usually get it all put away in a day."

"Oh." She hooks her bottom lip with her teeth for a second, looking uncertain. "Are you sure you don't want somebody to log where everything goes so you don't have to go door-to-door next year?"

I chuckle because she's not exaggerating by much. "Now that I'm actually in charge, most of it will be going in my barn."

"Okay. That's good, then."

After a painful moment of awkward silence, I decide to rip the bandage off. "I should have sent you a text, but I think we're all set."

That bland, polite business expression she wore the day I met her slips over her face like a mask. Then she nods once. "I'll get out of your way, then."

"Thank you for your help. It was a great fair." I'm grateful my voice doesn't crack as I force the words out. "I'll probably see you again before you go."

"Probably." Her smile is as stiff as her spine. "But if not, goodbye, Rob."

Those last two words are like a knife in my gut, but Whitney's gone by the time I get my breath back. I want to chase after her and spin her around before hauling her into my arms and never letting her go.

Instead, I walk to the bench and open the top of the coffee she brought me. I don't take a sip of it, though, because I'm honestly afraid I might cry if I do. Hopefully, someday I'll be able to drink a coffee Beth made without thinking of Whitney, but that day definitely won't be today. Or tomorrow.

Trying to throw myself into admin work doesn't do the trick, either. There aren't enough numbers or budget proposals or incident reports to distract me from the look in Whitney's eyes when I told her there wasn't any need for her to be here.

I'll probably see you again before you go.

My own words are killing me. What does that even mean? I'll see her as she drives away after an awkward, impersonal goodbye in front of my family? And then…she's just gone?

No. That's not okay.

Whitney's only been in my life for two weeks, so I should be able to wish her well and move on with my life. But right now, I can't even picture what my life will look like after she's gone. Every time I try to imagine showing up at family events or grabbing a burger at the diner, Whitney's with me. Trying to forcibly remove her from the mental picture doesn't work.

I *want* her with me.

I need to tell her that. I have to tell her it doesn't make any sense and I'd be asking her to sacrifice her life and career in the city, but I want her to stay and give us a chance.

And I need to tell her *now*.

Every minute that goes by is another minute that goodbye has had a chance to settle in and take hold.

I don't turn on the lights and siren. It's tempting, but if I'm seen careening into the inn's driveway, everybody in town will be worried about Natalie and the baby, and nobody needs that right now.

Instead, I pull into the driveway at a normal speed and shut off the SUV. I don't want to get slowed down by my family and they're most likely to be in the kitchen—though most of the vehicles are gone—so I don't go through the back door as I usually would. I jog around to the front of the house and up the steps, almost eating it on a slick spot that I make a mental note to salt later.

The front room is empty, as I'd hoped, and I go straight to the stairs. I'm halfway up when the loud thumping of my footsteps on the treads sinks in and I realize I still have my boots on. I'm not turning back now, so I add cleaning the floors after salting the steps to the to-do list I'm compiling in my head.

Getting to Whitney is number one on the list, though, and I'm not stopping until I find her.

Her door is ajar and swings open under my knock. I don't see her, even as I step inside. The bathroom door is open and the light is off, so she's probably not in there. For one horrible, heartbreaking moment, I think she's gone.

Then I see her suitcase on the floor next to the armoire. There's a notebook and pen on the nightstand, and her phone charger is still plugged into the wall. I inhale deeply, breathing in the faint scent of her, and will my heart rate to return to something near normal. It's not going to happen, though.

Whitney's not in the room, but she hasn't left. She's some-where in this town and I need to find her. But what if I go driving around looking for her, but I miss her and she comes back here and checks out before I circle back?

I go to the nightstand and flip to a clean page in her note-book. I'd tear the page out, but it's one of those bound jour-nal-type notebooks and if the whole thing unravels, there's a good chance she won't forgive me. There's also a chance she won't forgive me for scrawling a messy note in her very orga-nized notebook, but that's a chance I'm willing to take.

Don't leave before I find you.

I set the notebook open on the bed with the pen on top, where she's sure to see it. Then I uncap the pen and add one more word.

Please.

Then I retrace my steps until I'm back downstairs and have to decide where to go next.

I hear Nat laugh in the kitchen, and I assume she's on the phone. It's a long shot, but asking her if Whitney told her where she was going might save me some time in the long run. Since I still haven't taken my boots off, I also need to tell her I'll come back and clean up before Mom sees it or she'll start yelling at me. And then Donovan will give me hell for leaving messy floors for his pregnant wife.

When I turn the corner into the kitchen, Nat's still laughing, but she's not on the phone. She's sitting at the kitchen table.

With Whitney.

I come to an abrupt stop, my heart pounding. I thought I'd have some driving around time to figure out what I want to say to her, but she's here and I have no idea what words should come out of my mouth. They're not exactly lining up in the right order in my brain.

"You didn't take off your boots," Nat points out, because that's the sisterly thing to do. "Luckily, you're not making a mess of the kitchen floor because you stomped all the salt and sand off on the stairs."

"I need to talk to Whitney."

Natalie arches an eyebrow. "I should say so."

That's when I realize Nat may have been laughing when I walked into the room, but Whitney's nose is a little red and her eyes are puffy. She was crying very recently.

"I'm going to go check on Sam," my sister says, rising from her chair. "I put him down for a nap in Nana Jo's room so I wouldn't have to go up and down the stairs, and he should be waking up any time. If not, I might close my eyes for a minute or two."

Once she's gone and hopefully out of earshot, I pull the chair she vacated closer to Whitney and sit down. She's watching me expectantly, and I still have no idea where to start. "I wrote in your notebook."

"Oh." Her eyes widen for a moment before she shakes her head. "You know how I feel about my notebooks, but I don't think you had to drive all the way here to confess that sin."

"No, I wrote in it after I got here. Just now, upstairs."

"Why? What did you write?"

"I didn't know where you were, so I left a note asking you not to leave before I found you." I take a deep breath. "I didn't rip the page out, though. So…yeah."

"Rob, what's going on?"

"I don't want you to go." There. Those were the words I needed to get out.

She looks at me for a long time, and I try to brace myself for her reaction. I know she'll be kind because that's who she is, but she's never let me believe she'd give up her life to stay here. With a guy she's known for two weeks, even.

"Why?"

The words come out of my mouth before I give any thought to what I should say. "Because I love you and I know we haven't known each other very long and it doesn't make *any* sense, but I do know I'm totally in love with you and I don't want you to go because I don't want to live the rest of my life without you in it. And I needed you to know that."

In the space of a single heartbeat, Whitney is out of her chair and in my arms, straddling my lap the way she did in the sleigh. I wrap my arms around her as she buries her face in my neck and I can feel the moisture of her tears on my skin.

"It doesn't make any sense, but I am totally in love with you, too," she says when she finally lifts her head so I can see her face. "I don't want to go."

There is so much joy and hope coursing through my body, I'm actually trembling. "You don't? You're going to stay in Charming Lake?"

"I am. I mean, I'm going to leave because I have an apartment and an office and a bank and—whatever, all that—but I'm coming back."

"Will you be back by Christmas?"

"I'm going to spend Christmas with my mom." Her eyes well up with tears again and she tries to blink them away, but one escapes and I wipe it away with my thumb. "Being with your family has made me realize I never want another Christmas without her. Natalie already said next year, we'll just add her to the crowd here, but for this year, it's short notice and I also need time to wrap up...you know, the whole life I used to have."

"Wait, Natalie knows you're coming back?" I shift in the seat, getting more comfortable, and I tighten my arms when Whitney starts to stand. I won't be letting go of her for a while.

"That's what we were talking about before you got here, actually. Your family seems to have already guessed that maybe you and I are meant to be, so there have been *discussions*. And yes, Nat said it like that, with emphasis."

"I guess if she's already planning on your mom joining us next year, the consensus was positive?"

She smiles down at me, her eyes sparkling. "Yes. Donovan has already created a position for me in Charming Lake."

Okay, so rich guys could be a pain in the ass, but his brother-in-law wasn't half-bad. "What is it?"

"So, it doesn't really have an official title or job description yet, but basically his liaison between his foundations and the community, so everybody's needs are met. And anything he needs done when he's in town. Maybe some remote work."

"So you don't have to give up your career?" It just keeps getting better.

"I'll be giving up the career I thought I wanted, but I'll be doing a job that makes me happy." She brushes her fingertips over my jaw. "Most importantly, I'll have you. I mean, I'll have to give up being able to have pizza delivered at one in the morning, but you're worth it."

I grin, still trying to process that I'm the luckiest guy on the planet right now. "I can microwave a pizza at one in the morning and deliver it to you in bed if that helps?"

"I'll hold you to that. I hope to be back by the end of the year, though I might have to make a couple of trips back to the city. Do you have plans for New Year's Eve?" When I wince, she sighs. "Oh, I guess that's probably a pretty busy night for first responders."

"It's not usually too bad in Charming Lake, but it depends on the weather sometimes. But the guys and I usually stay at the station."

"That's okay. I know I'll be sharing you with the community, but I'll be waiting for you when you get…wait—"

"Yes, you're moving in with me," I tell her. "As a matter of fact, I'll go upstairs right now and get your stuff and drive it to my house so it's official, so when you leave, you're leaving from there."

She laughs and then I can't take it anymore. I cup the back of her neck and draw her down for a long, thorough kiss that makes everything right in my world again. Then she rests her head on my shoulder and I just hold her.

"You know," I say after a few minutes. "I really thought we were going to end up on the naughty list for what we did on that sleigh, but Santa really came through on this one. Our own Christmas miracle."

WHITNEY
10 months later

"You are *not* dressing up as a firefighter for Trunk or Treat," I inform Rob as he descends the stairs in his CLFD T-shirt and uniform pants.

"I'm always a firefighter for Trunk or Treat."

"Because you're always a firefighter." I put my hands on my hips. "It's cheating."

He's not really paying attention to me until he hits the bottom of the stairs and looks directly at me. Then he stills, his gaze sliding down over my costume.

His brows draw together. "I thought you were going to be a super sexy and villainous fairy tale queen."

I laugh at his disappointment. "No, I showed you that costume and you said absolutely yes and then I snorted because, *actually*, absolutely not."

"So, you went with…" He waves his hand toward me. "That?"

"I'm a teddy bear," I say, putting my arms out. The fuzzy

one-piece costume even has a hood with little ears. "You wouldn't believe how warm and comfortable this thing is."

"Are you naked under it?"

"No." I laugh and slap his hand when he tries to feel my ass through the costume. "We have to go or we're going to be late."

We ride together in his SUV, as we always do. Only twice have I ever been stranded when he had to leave on an extended call, and once I went to the General Store and visited with Beth, and the other I walked to the inn and hung out in the kitchen with Penny.

Since the main street is closed off for the town's Halloween celebration, he parks next to a police cruiser and we walk the rest of the way. After giving me a kiss and a sneaky tug of my teddy bear's tail, he heads to the engine and his guys, while I head to the booth I'll be manning. Donovan was in town to take Sam trick-or-treating, and he'd set up earlier in the afternoon. Once I arrive, he'll join his wife and son—who is dressed as a blue dog from TV he's obsessed with—along with his adorable daughter, Becca, who is dressed as the blue dog's little sister for her first Halloween.

I'm representing Donovan's latest initiative, handing out information on how our neighbors can receive free winterization upgrades for their homes. And since I *might* have volunteered to be on the Trunk or Treat committee—and honestly, almost every committee in Charming Lake—I can see the fire truck from the spot I assigned my booth to.

The entire crew is present today, with neighboring departments ready to cover if an emergency occurs. The guys are wearing costume bunker coats over their T-shirts, not wanting to expose all the kids to their actual gear, though they're wearing their helmets. Watching Rob interact with his community always fills me with joy, and it's extra special now that it's *my* community, too.

By the time the kids going up and down the street to

collect candy is over, as well as the costume parade and awards and all the other fun activities, I'm regretting the teddy bear costume. The problem with choosing a costume that's warm enough to be able to skip a coat at the end of October in New England is that sometimes it's not that cold.

"Do you want me to put the AC on?" Rob asks when we're finally back in the SUV and I have my window halfway down.

"No, because it's not actually hot, so you'd probably have to set the thermostat to like forty degrees to make it kick on. I just want a little breeze on my face."

When he turns into our driveway and hits the button to open the door, I have a moment to appreciate that feeling of *home* that never gets old before we're pulling into the garage.

I love our home. Our life together. I own my own jeans now, the community of Charming Lake has made me one of their own, and I get to wake up every morning next to the love of my life—as long as he's not on a call.

"I can't wait to get out of this," I say once we're inside, but Rob stops my hand when I reach for the zipper.

"Hold on a sec. I'll be right back."

I laugh when he ducks into the kitchen and returns with the candy bowl we'll be using when the kids do their official Halloween neighborhood trick-or-treating in a couple of days.

"It's all your favorite candy. I picked out all the ones you don't like." I smile and reach for it, but he covers the candy with his other hand and pulls the bowl out of my reach. "What do you say?"

I laugh, but when he doesn't give in, I surrender. "Trick or treat."

When he removes his hand, there's a small velvet box nestled in the center of the candy. My hand goes to my mouth as I gasp in surprise.

After lifting the box out, he sets the bowl on the coffee table and opens the lid. The diamond winks at me—small and round and incredibly beautiful—before he plucks it from its satin pillow.

"I love you, Whitney. I fell head over heels for you the first day I saw you, and I fall more in love with you every day. Will you be my wife?"

"Yes," I whisper, tears clogging my throat. We'd talked about marriage, but in a vague way, like something we'd get to at some point. I never expected this, and after he slides the ring onto my finger, I throw my arms around his neck. "I love you so much. I can't wait to marry you."

He has to burrow under the fake fur to press a kiss to my neck. "You feel like a furnace in this thing."

"Be honest. When you imagined this, you thought you'd be proposing to a super sexy villain queen, didn't you?"

"The teddy bear works, too, but I kinda pictured it that way, yes," he says, and then he laughs and kisses me again.

Thank you so much for reading Rob and Whitney's story! If you enjoyed it, please consider leaving a review on the retailer's site to spread the word to other readers. If you missed Donovan and Natalie's romance, you can find Stranded In A Small Town Christmas here!

And please subscribe to my newsletter to get all the last news on sales and new releases, and turn the page for a complete list of my available books!

Also by Shannon Stacey

To see the most current list of titles by Shannon Stacey, visit the Books tab on her website, shannonstacey.com.

———

Standalone Contemporary Romances

The Kowalski Family Series

This reader-favorite contemporary romance series is full of family, fun and falling in love.

The Sutton's Place Series

Three sisters come together to open the family brewery so their mother doesn't lose everything, but they don't expect to find love along the way. Friends, family, love and laughter!

<u>Her Hometown Man</u> — Book 1

<u>An Unexpected Cowboy</u> — Book 2

<u>Expecting Her Ex's Baby</u> — Book 3

<u>Falling For His Fake Girlfriend</u> — Book 4

<u>Her Younger Man</u> — Book 5

<u>Married By Mistake</u> — Book 6

The Blackberry Bay Series

Feel good romances about love and laughter in a small town.

<u>More Than Neighbors</u> — Book 1

<u>Their Christmas Baby Contract</u> — Book 2

<u>The Home They Built</u> — Book 3

Cedar Street Novellas

Fun, tropey hijinks in a small town!

<u>One Summer Weekend</u> — Book 1

<u>One Christmas Eve</u> — Book 2

Hockey Romances

<u>Here We Go</u> — Book 1

<u>A Second Shot</u> — Book 1.5

The Devlin Group Series

This action-adventure romance series follows the men and women of the Devlin Group, a privately owned rogue agency unhindered by red tape and jurisdiction.

<u>72 Hours</u> — Book 1

<u>On The Edge</u> — Book 2

<u>No Surrender</u> — Book 3

<u>No Place To Hide</u> — Book 4

Holiday With A Twist

Hold Her Again

Feels Like Christmas

Standalone Novellas

Through the Rain

Heart of the Storm

Slow Summer Kisses

Kiss Me Deadly

Historical Western Rom Coms

Taming Eliza Jane — Book 1

Becoming Miss Becky — Book 2

Subscribe to Shannon's newsletter

About the Author

New York Times and *USA Today* bestselling author Shannon Stacey lives in New Hampshire with her family. Her favorite activities are writing romance and really random social media posts with her dog curled up beside her, especially during the long winter months. She loves books, coffee, Boston sports, watching way too much TV, and she's never turned down an offering of baked macaroni & cheese.

📘 facebook.com/shannonstacey.authorpage

📷 instagram.com/shannonstacey

🦋 bsky.app/profile/shannonstacey.bsky.social

🧵 threads.net/@shannonstacey

Made in the USA
Columbia, SC
15 December 2024

49439558R00085